AMONG FRIENDS

A Quaker Boy at the Battle of Plattsburgh

by Stephen B. Woodruff

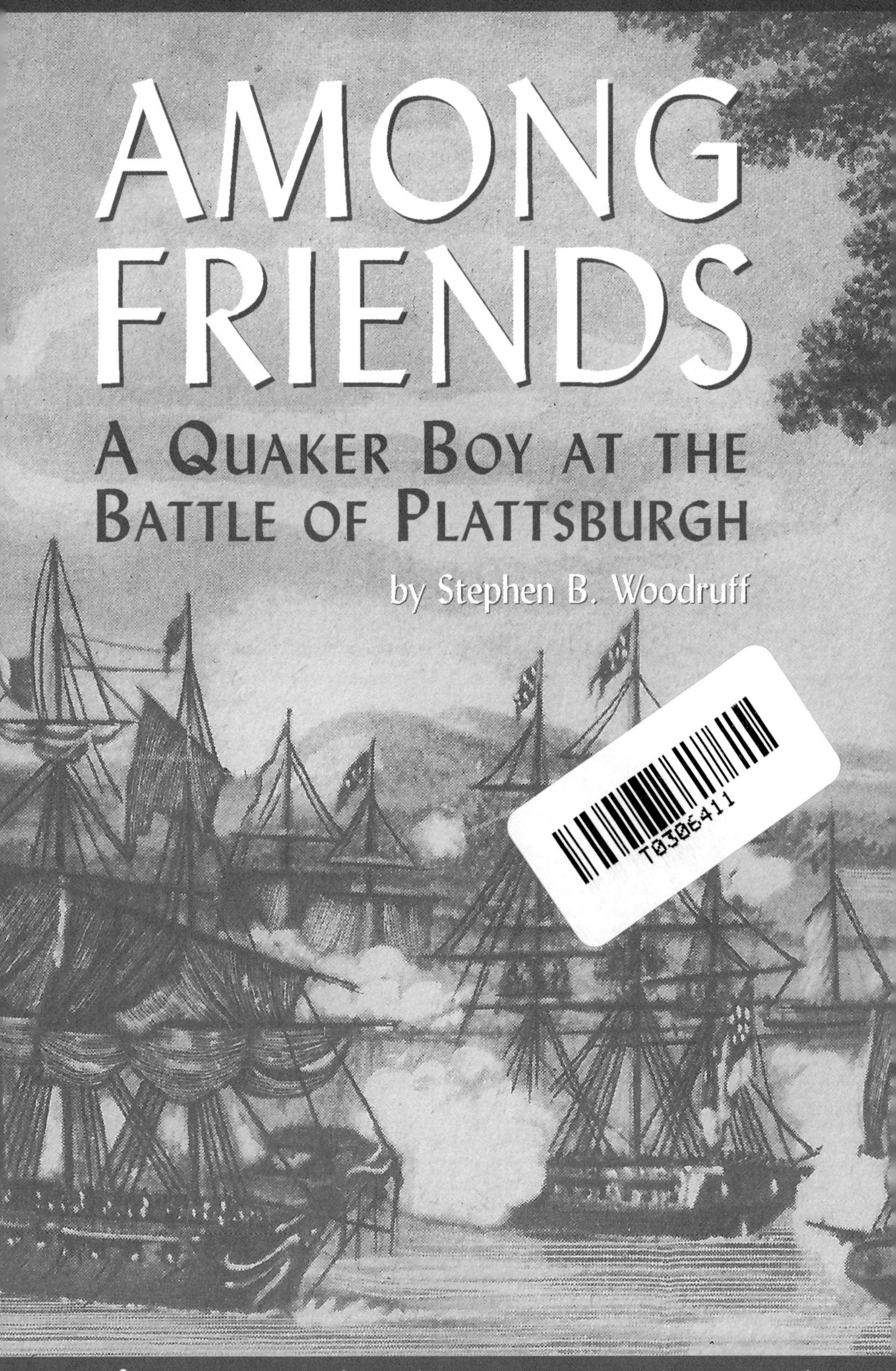

North Country Books · Utica, New York

ISBN-10 1-59531-044-4
ISBN-13 978-1-59531-044-6

Design by Zach Steffen & Rob Igoe, Jr.

Cover Illustration: Macdonough's Victory on Lake Champlain,
B. Tanner Print, From the collections of the Clinton County
Historical Association

Library of Congress Cataloging-in-Publication Data in Progress

North Country Books, Inc.
220 Lafayette Street
Utica, New York 13502
www.northcountrybooks.com

To my family, with love and thanksgiving

ACKNOWLEDGMENTS

I would like to thank fellow authors and mentors Ned McIntosh and Kristi Collier who offered criticism and advice, both for the article I published some years ago about Aikin's Volunteers, and for the manuscript that has become *Among Friends*.

Thanks go to the members of the Battle of Plattsburgh Commemoration Committee who have put forth tireless efforts for sixteen years to produce an annual, week-long celebration commemorating the event and entertaining the public—but more than that, educating all who attend about the importance of the battle on September 11, 1814. The educational materials they have generated over the years have been invaluable in writing the story with historical accuracy.

I am grateful to my friend Gary VanCour (co-chair of the Commemoration Committee), retired teacher and historian, for encouraging me to purchase the journal of H.K. Averill at its publication. Our many conversations over the years have provided the background knowledge needed to frame the story.

Thanks to Ron and Carol Allen, historians for the

town of Peru, New York, who oversee a wonderful collection of Peru's historical memorabilia. They have preserved, in photographs and written documents, the stories of Old Peru, and the lives of the Quaker people who founded the settlement. These materials prompted the underlying question: "What would happen if a Quaker boy from the Peru Union became involved with Aikin's volunteers?"

I am indebted to Rob Igoe, Jr., Zach Steffen, and the staff at North Country Books for bringing the manuscript to its final form, and for their careful readings and suggestions along the way.

Finally, thanks to my wife, Jeanette, for suggesting I embark on this writing journey in the first place, and to my children, who, whether they know it or not, continue to provide inspiration and a reason to write.

FOREWORD

Among Friends *is a work of historical fiction featuring a young Quaker boy living in a settlement near what is today the village of Peru, NY. To help readers understand certain story events, the author offers some history and background about Quakers and their lifestyle.*

The Quakers, known also as "Friends of the Light" or "Friends of the Truth" (later the "Society of Friends") were founded by George Fox in England in the seventeenth century. Quakerism grew out of the Protestant Reformation in England. The Friends viewed their movement as a third branch of Christianity, different than Roman Catholics or Protestants. They separated from the Church of England, believing it was too dependent on material things, excessive decorations, doctrines, and procedures. They desired a more mystical experience of God, a personal, spiritual Presence, requiring neither church nor priest nor book.

The Church of England persecuted Quakers. They were imprisoned or had their land and possessions taken away. They sought refuge in the New World, coming to the Massachusetts Bay Colony in the late 1600's, where they were persecuted as dangerous heretics by the Puritans—they were deported, imprisoned, or hanged. Governor Winthrop drove them out of the colony, and they moved to West Jersey in 1675 and to Pennsylvania in 1682. They also settled on Long Island and in the region of Duchess County in New York. The Quakers who founded the Peru Union in the late 1700's originated there.

The Quakers formed communities to retain their identity and avoid the influence of "world's people." Country Quakers, like the people in *Among Friends*, built towns and operated farms and related businesses or trades. They were kind, hardworking, trustworthy people as described by others.

To further set themselves apart, Quakers used "thee" and "thy" in their speech, words which had begun to disappear in English by that time. This, to them, was a type of "plain speech." It was also grammatically unique, using "thee is" rather than "thou art," derived from a speech pattern common in the Yorkshire region of England. Quakers today seldom, if ever, use this pattern of speech.

Quaker clothing exhibited simplicity and plainness. Men wore a hat and refused to remove it in the presence of authority figures. The hat was usually gray and broad-brimmed with a rounded or flat crown. Their shirts, for work and formal dress, had neither collars nor buttons. Women wore a long, dress, covered by a cape or kerchief, fronted by an apron, and a bonnet.

Black shoes and stockings were the rule. They wore no make-up or jewelry. Quakers believed their outward dress should reflect inward quietness of the spirit.

Country Quakers at the time of this story made their living by subsistence farming, producing most of the goods they needed and growing and raising most of their own food. Many operated sawmills and gristmills. A Quaker man might be a house wright, carpenter, blacksmith, or breeder of stock—any occupation important to the group's well-being.

Quakers accepted the core beliefs of Christianity, but emphasized the importance of the Holy Spirit in uniting the group as a whole. There were no rites or sacraments or liturgy. Quakers simply sought the Inner light in silence together—a kind of group mysticism. They believed Inner Light, "that of God," existed in all people and rendered them equals. Men and women had the same value before God; women were encouraged to minister to others and to speak out in church when the Spirit moved them. Quaker meetings for worship, usually two per week, were held in silence; no one spoke unless they believed they had received a Truth worth sharing.

Quaker lives were simple and plain. They rejected violence or killing or war. They lived by testimonies of peace, integrity, equality, and simplicity. They avoided alcohol and profanity. They abhorred slavery and worked in the Abolitionist movement. They refused to swear oaths against a fellow human being.

The community insisted upon strict adherence to this

way of life. Overseers from the group would report failures in conduct they witnessed. The accused would have to "make satisfaction" to the meeting and change for the better—or they could be "disowned."

Quaker communities disappeared over time in part because so many members were disowned for one offense or another. Many Quaker men and women married non-Quakers, appeared out of plain clothing, took part in musical or other social events. Some were seen in drunken condition or spent too much time in taverns or other "places of diversion." The opening of western territories and the promise of fertile land also led to the abandonment of many Quaker settlements.

From 1800 to 1827, tensions grew among the members of the Society due to the preaching of Elias Hicks, a Long Island Quaker with a more mystical approach to Quakerism. Many of his beliefs were seen as unchristian by traditional Quakers. Communities divided, with some choosing to be Hicksite, and others Orthodox. This did little to encourage the unity so central to Quaker belief.

The Society of Friends exists in modern times, with 130,000 members in the United States and 250,000 worldwide. Though the most identifying features of speech and dress have been largely discontinued, their core belief in the Inner Light that draws them closer to God and to one another remains.

CHAPTER ONE

First Day, September 4, 1814

Nothing stirred Elijah Hoag's memory like silence. On this sweltering September day, the oppressive calm of the Quaker meetinghouse smothered him. The quiet, meant to draw the members of the Society of Friends into communion with God, instead pushed Elijah farther away. But he had no trouble filling the void with other thoughts.

Men and boys sat on rough-hewn pine benches, dressed in First Day meeting clothes—coats and pants in shades of gray and light brown, with matching hats on their heads. The simple, white, collarless shirt Elijah wore under his coat was soaked with sweat, its loose, homespun fabric scratching his skin. A trickle of perspiration emerged from under the hat and rolled down aside his ear. All around the room eyes were closed, heads bowed ever so slightly. The Friends were deep in prayer, in unity with the Inner Light. On the other side of the low partition, the women would be in the same attitude. The Quakers of the Peru Union drew personal power from the quiet of the meeting, connected to the indwelling Christ, unified as a community. It was the

Quaker way. But more and more, it was not Elijah's.

Today Elijah was drifting far from the Light, far from the bulky bodies pressed against him on the rough pine bench. Praying was impossible. His head pulsed with the unshakeable memory of two days ago. Two days since the most recent failure in his long litany of failures. Two days since he was reminded about his lack of skill and judgment, about the disappointment he was becoming to his family.

The wagon had been clipping along the Rogers Road, wheels fairly singing, accompanied by the rhythmic gait of Esther and Ruth, the Vermont-bred horses who'd come to the Champlain Valley as colts with Elijah's parents years ago. The chestnut mares were proficient whether saddled or hitched to a harness, and today they pulled with joy. The wagon held sacks of freshly ground corn from the gristmill at Goshen, plus sugar from Elmore's store in Peru Village. They were headed south, bound for home.

Elijah let the horses have their way on the well-known route to the Union. He squinted into the late morning sun, seeing in his mind's eye the wondrous mechanism of the water-driven gristmill. It amazed him how the steady flow of the Little Sable River could turn the great millstone brought to Goshen fifteen years ago from Duchess County by the mill's owner, John Keese. The intricate system of levers and gears intrigued him—such technological advances had allowed his family and others like them, Quaker and non-Quaker, to carve a thriving settlement out of the virgin forest in the space of thirty years. Gristmills, sawmills, a tannery, dry goods stores, hotels—all anyone could need or want was provided in this year of 1814 in the township of Peru, New York.

As he rode along, Elijah recalled, too, the troubling dreams he'd had the last few nights—vivid dreams whose images he couldn't shake off. His town, the Peru Union, its houses and shops, the surrounding farms—gone—destroyed. Broken buildings, a neglected cemetery, and the ruins of the meetinghouse were the only evidence a thriving community had existed there. The two Lombardy poplars in whose shade the townsfolk often gathered were stripped of their leaves and branches, and they stood like silent skeletons, sole witnesses to some great devastation. Elijah shuddered and shook his head to rid it of the awful vision. The dreams frightened him. His father's cousin, Joseph, frequently had visions, and some of them had come true. Elijah wondered if his nightmares might do the same.

As he neared their gate, Elijah looked over his shoulder. A dust trail rose in a brownish cloud. The wagon seemed to stand still, and Elijah noted the fields of golden wheat, newly-cut, edged by the deep green of pines. The nearby hills were spotted with the red of maples and yellow of aspens, signs of the season's turn. The distant, blue-tinged mountains opened their arms and embraced this wide, flat valley on Lake Champlain's western shore. For a moment, Elijah stopped thinking about the dreams, so caught up was he with the magnificence of his home.

A jerk on the reins jolted him out of his reverie. In their eagerness, Esther and Ruth had accelerated as they approached the lane. Elijah whirled around, but the loosely held reins had slipped from his hands. Instead of turning at the gate, the mares left the hard-packed dirt drive and clattered into the Hoag's wheat field. Elijah lurched forward and toppled headfirst over the footrest. Tails swishing, the horses nibbled at the tops of the grain, content to have found food so soon after the pull from town. Elijah looked up to see his father running toward him and could hear his sister Rebecca's delighted laughter at the back door.

"How many times must I tell thee," his father snapped, throwing down the scythe he was carrying. "Keep both thy hands on the reins and thy face forward. This Morgan breed is spirited. If they don't feel a firm hand, they'll go their own way. Are thee hurt?" he asked, unhitching the horses.

"No, Pa," Elijah had answered. Not physically, at least.

But Rebecca's giggling continued, and she braced herself against the door frame until she regained her composure. "Elijah, there is plenty of wheat to go around! Why not join Esther and Ruth and eat thy fill after the long day?" Her laughter erupted again as she disappeared into the house, closing the half door. Rebecca seemed to take great delight in torturing him lately.

"A shock or two of wheat ruined because of thy carelessness!" his father said, shaking his head. "Must I send Jeremiah to do thy work? Thee is fourteen now! When can I depend on thee to shoulder thy share?" Elijah cringed at the thought of his brother, two years younger, sent to do his work.

Elijah shook his head to rid it of the memory. He looked around the room. There was deep silence in the meetinghouse—how much time had passed? Elijah relished the silence, in a way. Here at least no one belittled or corrected him. No one saw humor in his failures. Rebecca, who regularly teased and poked fun at him, sat out of sight behind the partition, alone today, since their mother had been so sick these last weeks with fever—too sick to come to meeting. "I shall wait upon the Lord here," she had said that morning. "We shall find each other just as well." Rebecca had assumed most of the household duties, and Elijah grudgingly admitted that running the house, preparing the meals, caring for their mother—all were big responsibilities for a girl just sixteen years old. Elijah worried about his mother, afraid her health might worsen, afraid to face life without her. He longed to see her well—they all did—once again organizing the daily hum of life at their farm. But for now, said the doctor, all they could do was let her rest and see if the fever passed.

Elijah surveyed the plain interior of the meetinghouse. It was without decoration, without ornaments. There was nothing to distract. Large windows with panes of wavy, locally manufactured glass obscured the view but allowed in the light—the only light Elijah felt at the moment. Inner Light, so prized by the Quakers, eluded him. Even Jeremiah, beside him on the bench, seemed to be deep in meditation. Squeezed in against his younger brother's side, Elijah felt small and weak. Jeremiah already could outwork Elijah—and out-pray him, too, it seemed.

His older brother, Israel, sat to his right. He was nearly as big as their father, with large, rough hands resting on his knees, eyes squinted shut, lips barely moving. Next to him sat Benjamin Hoag, a gentle giant of a man, a fact for which Elijah was grateful, especially lately, given all his blunders. Again and again he had failed to live up to his father's hopes.

Ben Hoag was deep in the faith and well respected in the meeting. He had great pride in his family's blessing, a gift of prophecy that surfaced every other generation or so. Ben believed Israel would receive the gift next, devout as he was. Looking at his brother, five years his senior, "deep down in prayer," as the elders said, Elijah wished with all his heart Israel would be the one. But these strange dreams of his! What could they mean? What if he, Elijah Hoag, had the gift? He could think of nothing he wanted less.

Years ago, his father's cousin Joseph, working in the fields, had experienced a vision predicting great strife among the Quakers. It seemed to Elijah the vision might be coming true. A difference of opinion was surfacing among the adults in the community. Methodism had begun in America and had taken root in Peru Village. Many of its central teachings—the sacredness of Scripture, the divinity of Christ, the personal salvation offered to believers in his name—had entered the spirit of the Quaker meeting, and many Friends embraced them wholeheartedly.

Other Friends still believed in a quiet, mystical pursuit of Inner Light—"that of God" within them. They accepted differences in the community as each person followed his or her own way. They wanted to retain the freedom of the early days, where there was less judgment, not so many rules. Elijah and Jamie Green, friends since they were little boys, frequently discussed their beliefs, but whenever they did, Elijah always ended up more confused.

Ben Hoag, though, had been clear about his feelings. He claimed a renewed richness in seeking the Light thanks to the new spirit in the meeting; he eyed with suspicion anyone who didn't share his point of view.

But Elijah couldn't say with assurance he'd ever felt connected to the Inner Light. So often he sat in meeting with his eyes squeezed tight, trying to see or feel something, some Other presence. It seemed so easy for his father and for Israel. Not only was Elijah not much of a farmer, he feared he wasn't much of a Quaker, either.

Something moved along the north wall—a cat—and it caught Elijah's eye. Seated ahead one row, Jamie Green leaned back and grinned. The others were so deep in meditation they were unaware. Jamie nodded toward the wall, signaling to Elijah he should watch.

The cat lived at the meetinghouse. The children would chase her before and after meeting, but she was aloof and uninterested in human contact. Her main interest was the mice living in and under the large, square structure.

A cracked earthenware pitcher sat on the floor along the wall. Elijah had a clear view of it. The cat nosed around, then poked her head inside the pitcher and placed her front paws on its rim as if to climb in. Elijah heard the scrape of her claws and a soft clunk as the pitcher struck the plank floor. A mouse skittered out and ran along the wall. The cat whirled as if to give chase, but stopped; her head was stuck inside.

Elijah looked to his left and right. Not a soul had noticed, except Jamie, of course. His wide grin indicated great enjoyment of this diversion from meditation. The cat danced sideways; the pitcher waved to and fro, looking every bit as if it had grown legs. She reared, suddenly airborne, as if to leap out of her prison, but instead drove the pitcher further over her shoulders. Jamie bit his fist to stifle a laugh. Elijah held his breath and covered his mouth with his hand. He could feel his ears burning with the strain of suppressing his laughter. The cat, her soft paws making only the slightest scraping sound, twirled, trying to spin out of her prison. Elijah saw Jamie bend over, his shoulders shaking, and he could bear it no longer. He exhaled, and then drew in air with a tremendous snort just as the cat and pitcher slammed the wall. The pottery shattered, and the cat, terrorized, sprinted down Elijah's row and leapt into his lap.

The gathering, as if on a signal, surfaced from their

meditation and turned toward Elijah. Jamie sat bolt upright, facing the front of the room. Disturbing the quiet of meeting was unthinkable, a point driven home since their youth. Without words, the people, some shaking their heads, stood to leave. The abruptness was unsettling. One elderly man in the row ahead turned and said, “Hasn’t thy father taught thee better behavior in the meeting, young Elijah?”

Ben Hoag reached across and rested his massive, work-hardened hand on Elijah’s knee, and Elijah felt the weight of it. “Get thee outside, Elijah Hoag,” his father said.

The cat in Elijah’s lap began to purr.

CHAPTER TWO

Elijah avoided eye contact with the clusters of Friends exiting the meetinghouse, but he felt their stares and sensed their disapproval as he wound his way down the side aisle toward the men's front door. The women were filing out the door on their side of the room, Rebecca among them. She looked at Elijah over the partition. "What has thee done this time?" she whispered.

Ignoring her, Elijah burst outdoors. He looked back and saw his father and brothers step into the doorway. His father's bulk filled the entrance. Benjamin Hoag scanned the groups outside until his gaze met Elijah's. Elijah felt his ears burning, his throat going dry. The cat had followed him and now wove herself around his legs, rubbing her face on his stockings, her purring a pleasant rumble vibrating against his ankles. His father opened the plain wooden door further so he could maneuver around people who had paused to greet one another. He adjusted his broad-brimmed hat and strode toward Elijah.

Jamie, still grinning, ran up to stand beside Elijah. "I see thy friend followed thee here," Jamie said. At

Jamie's words, the cat skittered away behind the meetinghouse.

"Not now, Jamie Green. Thee had better go."

Benjamin Hoag drew near, stared a long moment at Jamie Green, then turned to his son. "Thee is aware of why we go to meeting, Elijah. Thy behavior brings shame to us and to thyself. Thee has been brought up to respect the time we wait on the Lord."

"Yes, Pa," Elijah answered. He pulled his hat further over his eyes and stared at his father's massive boots. Proper behavior in the meeting had been required of him from the time he was small. His father expected him to know better. "I'm sorry," he said.

Ben Hoag rested his hands on Elijah's shoulders, and Elijah raised his eyes to meet his father's. Ben's face showed no anger, only a calm sadness. "We come together on the first and fifth days to seek the Lord, Elijah, to feel his light within us, to be one together, as believers. It is a sacred time, not meant for fool's behavior." Elijah could feel the serious intent behind his father's gentle words. He frequently received these soft reproaches. Elijah sometimes wished for genuine anger from his father, a torrent that would come, then be forgotten, like a summer cloudburst. It was so much harder to endure the subdued but constant rain of his father's correction.

Ben Hoag inhaled deeply and sighed. Elijah sensed what was coming. He had heard it before. "Pay attention to thy brothers and how they conduct themselves—even young Jeremiah," Ben said. "They find their way into prayer and thee must do the same. Thee must be more meditative—thee must think on the scripture; thee must meditate on our Lord, the incarnate God, and contemplate his atoning sacrifice on our behalf." Ben squeezed Elijah's shoulder. "To face the trials of this world, Elijah, we must seek strength from the Source that is greater than ourselves." He turned to look at Jamie Green. "Beware anyone who would lead thee astray and violate the sanctity of the meeting. Some who call themselves Friends are listening to ancient voices, drawing us away from Jesus and his sacred word. Mark my words; there will come a day when they will acknowledge this new spirit among us."

Elijah looked at Jamie, who was shifting from one foot to another, cheeks reddened, eyes angry. Usually Ben Hoag expressed his unhappiness about the Greens while working at home. This was the first time he had spoken his feelings in public, in front of a Green.

Ben had long been at odds with the preaching of Elias Hicks, a Long Island farmer whose interpretation of scripture and beliefs about Christ the Light hearkened to an earlier time, and the Greens, Ferrisburgh Quakers, were influenced by Hicks eleven years ago when he visited their Vermont town. Brother Hicks was a powerful speaker, and the Greens still embraced his words. They had come to the Union when Jamie and Elijah were small and did not shy away from sharing their viewpoints. Ben was angered by how these newcomers disrupted the unity and encouraged division in the community. He viewed the Greens and others like them with a wary and critical eye.

Israel and Jeremiah sidled up to their father. Israel turned to gaze north up the Rogers Road toward Goshen and Peru Village. Nothing made Elijah feel more out of place than standing with his brothers, both of whom were the image of their father—Israel, nineteen and powerfully built; Jeremiah, like a miniature of his father and oldest brother, yet taller and stronger than Elijah, more suited to the hard physical labor of subsistence farming, where every member of the household must help attain the basic necessities of food, clothing, and shelter.

Their arrival broke the tension of the moment. Ben Hoag smiled at Israel and Jeremiah. "A cantankerous cat couldn't keep thee from seeking the Lord," Ben proclaimed with pride. "Isn't that so, Israel…Israel?"

Israel turned abruptly, as if startled. "I'm sorry, Pa. I didn't hear thee."

"Where did the cat go, Elijah?" asked Jeremiah.

"'Round behind the meetinghouse," replied Elijah, and his younger brother headed off in that direction.

"What cat are you talking about?" Israel asked.

Ben's smile grew broader. "Now that's going down deep! Mark well the way to meditate, Elijah. When you are in the Light, nothing should intrude." Israel's puzzled look remained, and he continued gazing up the road. Ben's smile faded as a voice called, "Benjamin Hoag, a word if thee please." A tall, slender man approached. It was Jamie's father.

"Samuel Green. What can I do for thee?" Benjamin

Hoag crossed his arms and regarded Jamie's father without expression.

"Benjamin, I am in the market to buy stock, and since thy reputation is second to none in the valley, I should like to purchase several head from thee."

"But what of thy own cattle, Samuel?" asked Benjamin.

"I made a number of sales recently and I need to bring my numbers back," Samuel Green replied. Elijah remembered Jamie speaking about a buyer from Vermont who had expressed interest in several head of the Green's herd. Elijah had thought nothing of it at the time, but Ben Hoag had raised an eyebrow when he heard the buyer was from Vermont.

"Is this another Vermont buyer after our good New York beef, or is there some other destination for the cattle?" Ben Hoag asked, an edge to his voice.

"What do you mean?" Samuel Green returned.

"What I mean is that in this time of war, there are Vermont farmers who are supplying the British army on our doorstep with meat on the hoof."

"Business is business, Benjamin. How the buyer disposes of the cattle he buys is of no concern to me, or to thee, for that matter," Samuel Green said, his voice rising. "I offer a quality product at a fair price according to our testimony of integrity. Besides, there is an American army and militia in Plattsburgh needing sustenance. Word has it the British are advancing toward the town. Surely in an extreme case as this thee can see how we must put aside our pacifist stand and do what is right for the good of this country?" Elijah glanced at Jamie, who was beginning to look as uncomfortable as Elijah listening to this tense exchange. It was rare to see Benjamin Hoag's temper, but this was the topic that stirred him.

"Samuel Green, as a newly appointed overseer in this meeting, it is my concern if Peru Union cattle, especially my own, are used to feed any army. This war is incited and conducted by world's people—it is not for us. Feeding soldiers, especially the enemy of this nation, is blasphemy, and challenges the peaceful tenet of our lives. We are charged to remain separate, uninvolved with the business of killing our fellow man. Thee cannot pick and choose what thee believes according to thy own will."

"The meeting has overstepped its bounds," countered Samuel Green. "It has no business meddling in my private affairs, nor do thee, whether thee is an overseer or not. I am weary of legalisms and laws invented by this meeting."

"I tell thee this," returned Ben Hoag. "At the time of our next monthly meeting we will pay thee a visit, Samuel Green, to see if it is indeed too late to save thy place in this fellowship."

"Disownment does not frighten me, for I'll not be alone," Samuel said, his voice rising in volume. "Others here in the Union share my beliefs."

Elijah was grateful that Rebecca, drawn by their voices, touched her father's arm. Sarah Green, Jamie's sister, accompanied her. Sarah stood by her father and said, "Father, thy voice is so loud!"

"Thee is right, Sarah," said Samuel Green. "There will be another time to discuss this. And as for stock, there are others with whom to do business."

He turned and strode toward his waiting wagon. Jamie followed.

Ben Hoag watched them go and then turned to his children. "Time to hitch the horses. Israel! Jeremiah! Lend a hand."

Sarah Green smiled at Elijah. "I'm coming later today to quilt with Rebecca. I hope I will see thee." She had large brown eyes and sandy hair that peeked from under her white bonnet. Elijah had known her for as long as he could remember. When they were younger, she was Jamie's pesky little sister, always around the boys in their work and play. They had looked forward to the time when she would start spending more time with Jamie's mother.

But lately Elijah felt differently about Sarah. He liked when she came to work at quilting or at the loom with Rebecca. He enjoyed talking with her, though he felt nervousness in his stomach when she smiled at him, as she was now. Elijah noticed Rebecca, head tilted to one side, watching, an amused look on her face.

"Well, I'll be home," said Elijah, "but I'll have work to do in the fields."

"It's first day, Elijah," said Rebecca. "Thee knows it will be a quiet afternoon until evening barn chores."

"Uh, yes, I forgot," said Elijah, shifting his feet and looking away down Rogers Road toward their farm.

"Perhaps I will see thee, then." Across the yard he noticed his father looking in their direction.

"I hope so," said Sarah, touching the sleeve of his coat before turning to go. "Good-bye, Rebecca."

"I will see thee later this day. Do not forget thy quilting needles this time!" Rebecca called. Elijah stood watching Sarah run toward her father and brother, who had hitched a horse to a small carriage. His stomach would have nearly stopped jumping, if he hadn't known Benjamin Hoag had been watching from a distance.

"Honestly, Elijah, must thee be such a goose all the time?" asked Rebecca, turning to him, smiling. "Sarah is my friend, 'tis true, and she comes to quilt with me or work the loom, but all she wants to talk about is thee. 'Where is Elijah today?' she asks, and 'What is he doing? Will he come back soon?'" Rebecca was enjoying this, Elijah could see.

"Elijah...Rebecca," boomed their father's voice. "Get to the wagon." As they climbed on, Ben continued. "Thee should learn to choose friends with more care. The ideas they embrace infect us like the pox. Disease will spread, then sicken and destroy us."

As their wagon rolled out of the meetinghouse yard, Elijah watched the Green's carriage turn down the Rogers Road. Sarah looked back and lifted her hand. Elijah felt his stomach jump again, but waved ever-so-slightly in return. Ben Hoag, hands on the reins and attention on the team, did not see. Israel gazed out at the fields. Jeremiah chattered about the cat. But Rebecca nudged Elijah with her elbow and smirked.

CHAPTER THREE

Second Day, September 5, 1814

Elijah wiped the sweat from his forehead and rested a moment, watching his father and younger brother make another sweep across the yellow-green hayfield. Ben Hoag swung the wooden-handled scythe in a giant arc, toppling the hay on the stubbly field. Jeremiah, walking alongside his father, matched his pace, striding with a rhythmic gait. At this rate, they would cover four acres today.

It was Elijah's job to follow with a long rake, gathering the hay into piles they later would load on wagons destined for the haymows. The rain last night had stayed to the north; they had seen thick blue clouds and flashes of lightning on the northern horizon. Distant thunder rumbled. But the Union had seen no rain, and now that the morning dew had burned off, the rising sun began to bake the land and the people who worked it. It was a prime haying day, though undeniably hot for ninth month, and it was difficult to harvest in the thick, humid air. Elijah kept hoping Rebecca might appear with a pitcher of cool water from the well, but she did not. Since her mother's illness, she had little time to think of much besides the housework, the cleaning chores, the regular preparation of meals.

"Mind, Elijah. Thee falls too far behind us. The rake is meant as a tool of work, not a leaning post," called Ben.

"Do thee wish to trade with me, Elijah?" offered Jeremiah. "I could take my time with the rake and thee could handle the scythe." Elijah cringed at the thought. His arms hadn't the length of Jeremiah's, and his past attempts at scything the hay had been unsuccessful, if not embarrassing. Rebecca had once observed, "Elijah, when thee works the scythe it looks as though thee may be trying to cut off thy foot!"

"Thank thee, no, brother," Elijah replied. "I'll catch up soon enough." His shoulders had begun to ache, and his hands were blistered and sore from sliding along the gray, weathered handle. He struggled to close the gap. Elijah couldn't escape the thought that after haying, a field of oats awaited, then several acres of wheat. The tool of choice for that job would be the cradle, like the scythe but with a set of wooden teeth that captured each swathe of grain and made the business of shocking easier. The cradle took more skill and strength than the scythe, so Elijah would be relegated to tying the shocks. Israel had great skill with the cradle, so at least Jeremiah would help him with the shocking. It sometimes took two people to wrestle the golden shafts into a bundle, tie them, stand them up, then move down the field to the next pile. The work never seemed to end.

Typically Israel would wield the scythe in the hayfield, and Jeremiah would help with the raking. But

Israel left after morning chores with a wagon full of corn to be ground into meal. Elijah was thankful when Benjamin Hoag paused at the end of a row and gestured northward up the Rogers Road, partially concealed by a rising cloud of dust. Elijah could make out a line of carriages and wagons coming their way.

"Even world's people know the value of a peaceful life, Elijah. Citizens of Plattsburgh,"—he gestured to the oncoming carriages—"are coming to the Union to escape the invasion. Thousands of British soldiers are assembled in Canada. The rumor is that they intend to follow the lake valley south, taking Plattsburgh as they pass by. There will be looting and burning. Cannon fire will destroy homes and lives. War is a curse on the earth, Elijah, and this war has been no better than any before it."

"But where will these people stay?" Elijah asked.

"Many have relations or acquaintances who live among us. The store once belonging to Henry DeLord has space to put up guests, and our inn will assist them. Some will continue up Hallock Hill to find refuge among the farmers there, taking shelter in their barns and buildings."

"But why here?" Jeremiah wondered.

"World's people know our attitudes about war. They know we'll not take aggressive action or invite violence. They feel it is safe here, and I pray it will remain so," Ben replied. He turned his attention to the uncut section of field. "Enough talk. Back to it, lads."

As he raked, Elijah thought about the impending

invasion he'd heard about on his errands to town. It was on everyone's mind. People worried that the British force would invade Peru Village on their push south, stealing provisions, wagons, horses—anything they would need to keep their army on the march. Elijah learned that Peru had formed a militia under command of David Cochran. At the time, he'd been ashamed to admit he didn't know much about this war, fought against Great Britain for two years now.

War frightened Elijah and fascinated him at the same time. The Friends spoke little about it, but he and Jamie had discussed it at length. Jamie seemed drawn to it, intrigued by the adventure, the chance to live so differently than their upbringing had taught. Jamie's family believed that in such a time as this, when a huge enemy force was poised against you, meeting force with force was justified.

Elijah wasn't so sure. Farm work was no attraction for him, but he liked the quiet, thoughtful ways of life among the Friends, safe from the concerns that troubled world's people, safe from the unspeakable violence of war. Elijah had learned to use a gun for hunting game, for protection against marauding animals. But the thought of using a gun to kill a fellow human being repulsed him. Still, encouraged by Jamie, he wondered what he would do, how he would react if he had to take a gun into battle.

The sweat on his hands stung the open blisters made by the rake, and he realized he had fallen behind again; Ben and Jeremiah were now a row ahead of him. Elijah began raking with renewed energy. Though his arms were weary, he knew he must do this job properly; he must impress upon his father that he was trying. He was thankful for the steady breeze across the fields that cooled his wet skin.

"That's it, Elijah," boomed his father. "Thee will yet become a farmer." It was a small compliment, but Elijah would take it. Ben Hoag did not offer encouragement often.

Elijah thought again how natural the farm work was for Jeremiah. His younger brother had helped with the chores from the time he could lift a bucket. But for Elijah, farming was a series of disasters, every season of the year, it seemed. Harrowing in the spring, walking behind Goliath and Samson, the mild-mannered oxen, Elijah had tripped and was dragged until Jeremiah arrived to help him. Later on, sections of the oat field had to be sown again because Elijah's scattering technique was found wanting—there were too many bare places where seed failed to fall. Sowing seeds was an art, sweeping the seed out of the shoulder bag, throwing, walking steadily—resulting in even coverage. Jeremiah, born to the task, took over the job. Elijah, though he respected his younger brother's natural abilities, resented having his work forever corrected and adjusted by him.

So Elijah was trying not to make mistakes today, and things were actually proceeding well. He had fed and watered the cattle in their enclosure, helped gather eggs, and cleaned up after milking. It was nearly dinner time now, the sun high in the sky—and there had been no major gaffes on his part! Elijah was agitated at Israel, gone since early morning. How long should it take to drive the wagon two miles to Goshen, unload the corn at Keese's gristmill, and drive home? Surely not several hours. Elijah missed the strong presence of his brother, who was fully able to carry his share of the work and some of his younger brothers' work as well. At least, he noted, Jeremiah and his father had nearly finished with the scythes; Jeremiah would be able to join him with the rake.

The sound of the dinner bell traveled across the short distance to the field, and Elijah imagined the fine lunch Rebecca would have ready to energize them for the afternoon's labor. But instead of three or four rings, the usual signal, the bell continued ringing, Rebecca striking it repeatedly eight, ten times. "Pa!" her voice drifted to them. "The stock is out of the pen and they're trampling the wheat!"

CHAPTER FOUR

It always amazed Elijah that for a large man, Benjamin Hoag could move with surprising speed. He dropped the scythe and sprinted toward the cattle paddock, Jeremiah right behind him. Elijah stood frozen in place, hand on his forehead, his mind racing. How could the cattle be in the wheat? How? How?! Hadn't he fed and watered them that morning? Hadn't he latched the heavy wooden gate? He gasped. As he had pulled the gate closed, Rebecca had yelled for help with the chickens. He must not have set the latch.

"Elijah," bellowed his father over his shoulder. "Get thee hence and help!" As Elijah ran, he saw Israel out of the corner of his eye, on the Rogers Road, nearly home. By the time he got to the field, Ben and Jeremiah, whistling and calling, had turned the herd and aimed it back toward the pen. Israel pulled up in the wagon, jumped out, and ran to help. Elijah got behind one brown-faced calf and pushed him toward the gate. The little animal was not easy to convince; he was contentedly munching the tips of the fragrant wheat. With effort, his shoulder pressing the animal's rump, Elijah aimed the bawling creature toward the line of cattle entering the pen. A final shove and he was inside with the others. Ben and Israel swung the heavy gate closed, fixing the latch with a loud snap. Ben turned to face his sons. Sweat poured down his face.

"Who cared for the stock this morning?" he asked, looking first to Israel, then to Elijah, then to Jeremiah. He returned his gaze to Elijah and stood in silence, as if he already knew the answer. Elijah's ears burned and his stomach had that queasy feeling. Behind his father, he could see the trampled wheat, stalks bent and broken, ruined. Once again, his ineptness had damaged crops and created trouble.

"I was out early this day, Pa," said Israel. "I loaded the wagon and left for Goshen and Peru Village." He looked up the Rogers Road toward the towns as if seeing something in the distance.

Elijah knew there was no use prolonging the questioning. "It was my job today," he confessed. "I must have left the gate open after morning chores."

"I am at fault, too," Jeremiah added. "When Rebecca called for Elijah's help with the chickens, he asked that I finish for him." Elijah glanced sideways at his younger brother. He had said no such thing.

"Elijah had a responsibility to do the job and not pass it off to thee," Ben said. "Now another quantity of wheat is of no use to us. When will thee learn how we depend on the wheat, and not just for ourselves, but to use for trade at the Yellow Store?" Ben paused, sighing deeply. "Everything we do, all our work, is to insure our survival in this place. Thee works against us, Elijah. Thee constantly falls short at thy tasks. I judge thee must be thankful to have Israel and Jeremiah who continually come to thy aid and properly finish thy work for thee. Pray God will help thee, Elijah. Perhaps that will give thee focus at fifth day meeting. Come. Rebecca has our dinner." Elijah stood in silence. Once again, despite his best attempts, he had failed. He was trying. Why wasn't God doing His part to help?

Ben trudged to the house, and Israel removed the harnesses from Ruth and Esther, leading them toward their stalls. "Go get the field tools and put them in the shed," he commanded his younger brothers. Elijah noted his brother's sharp tone. It was unlike him. Usually he was soft-spoken and understanding. He had been distant for weeks, it seemed, and short-tempered.

"Thee should not lie to protect me, Jeremiah," Elijah said as they returned to the place they'd stopped work.

"I heard Rebecca call and wondered if thee had closed the gate," said Jeremiah. "I should have checked."

"Tell no more falsehoods on my account, Jeremiah," said Elijah. "If Pa found out it would give him one more reason to be disappointed in me. But thee is a good brother…and friend."

"Things will improve," said Jeremiah. "Thee will see! The field work went without problem this morning." Elijah appreciated his brother's encouragement, but the truth was clear.

"A few hours of success does not balance my list of

failings," said Elijah. "I know farming is not for me. My failures make more work for thee and for Israel." Elijah wished he had been sent to deliver the corn instead of Israel that morning. He loved the grinding sound as the great millstone turned, crushing the wheat or corn, the fragrant, nutty aroma of the freshly ground grain filling the air. He could stand for hours and watch the clattering belts and gears turn the stone to make flour and meal. John Keese jokingly asked Elijah more than once if he wanted to learn a "real" trade instead, as he said, "of spending thy life walking behind oxen," but he always asked the question in Ben Hoag's presence; Ben's lack of comment told Elijah his father was not pleased at John Keese's attempt to lure him from the farm, whether he meant it or not. Elijah frowned. With the sweet smell of the freshly cut hay hanging in the warm air, they picked up the dropped scythes and returned to the house.

The back door of the clapboard farmhouse opened into the kitchen, usually a bustling place with Rebecca and their mother hard at work all day preparing meals. But with Mother sick, it was quiet—too quiet. It lacked the warm spirit, the quiet conversation, their mother's knowledge of how to run a house smoothly. Rebecca tried, but it just wasn't the same.

His sister had prepared dinner, the largest meal of the day, meant to fortify the men for their labor in the fields and curb the effects of the draining heat and humidity. On the table she had placed vegetables from the kitchen garden, fresh-bread from the cast iron Dutch oven, and two chickens she had roasted over the open-hearth fireplace, its yawning opening large enough to step into while cooking. Her mother had directed her from bed in the small adjoining room, too feverish yet to join the family. Rebecca added blue pitchers of milk and cold water, and cheese from the springhouse. The cooking fire radiated heat to the kitchen along with the scent of smoke. Ben Hoag sat at the rough-planked sawbuck table, more than sufficient for the meal, especially now, with their mother ill.

Elijah and Jeremiah joined their father. Israel arrived, drenched in perspiration after wiping down the horses, stabling them, and giving them grain and water. Rebecca moved quietly from the fireplace to the table, refilling plates as needed, sitting down only after the men slowed their eating. No one spoke. Elijah knew better. Though nearly fifteen, he was a child, and was not allowed an opinion on any topic unless asked.

Benjamin Hoag looked up from his empty plate. "All of us will need to finish the hay today, for wheat is due to be started on the morrow—what wheat there is remaining," he added, looking at Elijah in a meaningful way. "It must be cut, shocked, and gathered into the lofts. John Keese expects us soon with a load to grind. And the oats are not far behind, ripe for the cutting. This heat portends a change, and the change can only mean rain."

"Pa, if it please thee, I should like to go back to town today," said Israel. "I can take more of last season's corn to John Keese. It will make more room in the cribs for the new harvest. Jeremiah and Elijah can scythe and rake."

"I've told thee we need to finish the hay before a change in weather," said Ben. "One trip to town today is enough for thee. Ruth and Esther are willing to pull, but this heat is hard on them. Sack the corn and put it in the east barn. We can take it to town another time."

"But Pa, there is some other business to which I must attend, and I pray thee that…"

"I'll hear no more about town," Ben repeated, firmly but quietly. "The younger boys need thy guidance and thy strong back, Israel." Elijah breathed deeply, grateful his father had discouraged another several hours without Israel. His stinging hands and aching shoulders told him that the afternoon's work would be challenging enough. "You and Elijah go assemble the tools; Jeremiah will help his sister in the kitchen before joining us in the field."

"Yes, Pa," said Jeremiah, though the look in his eye betrayed to Elijah how he felt doing woman's work. Israel stood abruptly and left without a word. Elijah followed his older brother outside.

Israel stood on the small porch off the kitchen, looking up the Rogers Road. "I saw John Keese on my trip to town this morning," Israel began, still gazing up the two-mile stretch of road toward Peru Village. "He says he wants to talk to Pa about something. He is thinking of building a second mill downriver. The current is plenty swift, and the banks are situated to receive another mill wheel."

"Do thee think he means to offer me an apprenticeship?" Elijah wondered. "I always thought he jested when he said that in front of Pa."

"He made no comment," said Israel. "He only said he sees potential in the town and feels he needs to provide more service. He can go back to Duchess County and purchase millstones there, as he did the first time. Winter is coming, and he could make the trip then. Work on another mill could begin by planting time. He has already contracted for a load of bricks from Barker's factory in Goshen."

"I hope he might be considering me," said Elijah, hope bursting in his heart. "But planting time…It would leave thee shorthanded here."

Israel continued to stare up the road. "Thee is thinking too much of thy dreams, and not of thy responsibilities at home. Thee will be needed here more than ever before."

Well, if not about his becoming an apprentice, then why did John Keese wish to see his father? Elijah couldn't imagine any other reason. And why wouldn't Israel want him to go? Surely he'd had enough of Elijah's failings. Surely he couldn't stand the thought of his incompetent younger brother living on an adjacent farm, blundering his way through his entire life.

And Elijah knew deep in his aching bones that farming was not his way. But what was his way? Becoming a miller's apprentice? Or was that just a fleeting dream to carry him away from a life he couldn't master and a father who thought he was a bumbler? And what if he failed in the mill? Still…

"Thank thee, Israel, for telling me of this," Elijah said. "Perhaps I shall go to John Keese myself…and soon."

CHAPTER FIVE

Third Day, September 6, 1814

The next morning, after chores and breakfast, Elijah bumped along the back road to Goshen. He smiled at his good fortune. A hard rain the night before had doused the Peru Union, rendering fieldwork impossible until at least later in the day.

The best use of time, their father observed, was to send Elijah to the mill with the last few sacks of the preceding year's corn. Meanwhile, he, Israel, and Jeremiah would sharpen the cribs in preparation for the wheat harvest. Elijah had not mastered the art of using the sharpening stone. Israel had nearly begged their father to be the one to take the load, but Ben Hoag was firm. First, Israel's skill with the stone was needed, and then Ben expected him to make adjustments to the harnesses.

Grim-faced, Israel had carried sacks of corn two at a time, flinging them into the back of the wagon so they hit the bed and skidded against the backrest. He loaded two for every one Elijah managed to wrestle out of the east barn and drag to the back of the wagon. Elijah couldn't understand Israel's desire to go to town. His older brother had always preferred the work of the farm to doing business among world's people.

So, he, Elijah, was off to John Keese's gristmill. Now he would have an opportunity to speak with the miller about the apprenticeship. Without his father nearby, Elijah was convinced the old miller would be clear about his intentions. If it was true, after the harvest, Elijah would approach his father with the news.

Before Elijah left the farm, Ben Hoag had given his usual guidelines for controlling Esther and Ruth, so Elijah was paying particular attention to his driving. "Keep thy eyes front," Ben had said. "Thee knows these are spirited mares who need a firm hand." Elijah watched the countryside roll by as the pair pranced down the well-worn dirt road with all their usual enthusiasm, the fresh morning air in their nostrils.

The rain the night before had washed the thick heaviness out of the air—this morning was cool and clear. The fields and trees sparkled with clinging water droplets; like crystals, they intensified the gold of the fields, and magnified the reds and yellows that overshadowed the summer's tired green. The crisp air invigorated Elijah, increasing his excitement at the plan to speak to John Keese. What better indication of his readiness for an apprenticeship than willingness to make his own arrangements!

He might have taken the Rogers Road, the more direct route to Goshen, but instead turned Esther and Ruth down the back road, running northwest toward the river, winding him past the home of his Great Aunt Winifred Hoag, whose simple farmhouse stood at the outer edge of their property. An independent Quaker lady in her eighties, Aunt Winifred enjoyed her solitude there at the Union, but loved when Elijah dropped by to visit. She was devout, deep in the Light, yet held surprising views on many subjects. Elijah delighted in his time with her, and he felt he could ask her anything. Her opinion differed so from his father's predictable reactions to questions about the ways of the Friends. Today he had things he needed to discuss with her.

Elijah did not see his aunt as he entered the drive to her rough-hewn home—the same pioneer-style home she had inhabited since coming to the Union in 1795. But he saw movement along the hedgerow between the house and fields and realized it was Aunt Winifred, a tiny wisp of a woman, dressed as all Quaker women in a long, gray dress, draped by a shawl, a white cap on her head. She was bent at the waist, gathering a cluster of late-blooming daisies, her favorite flower. She looked up as he drew near to the house, smiling.

"Well, Elijah, dear one," she said. "Water thy horses and come help me with these daisies. There are so many I can't hold them all." She picked up the bottom edge of her white apron and dropped the handful of yellow-centered flowers into the fold.

"Yes, Aunt," said Elijah, hurrying off the wagon seat. He pumped water into a wooden trough fronting the rail where he tied the horses.

"Now," she said, pointing a bony, blue-veined hand toward the spot, "go to that patch over there and pick as many daisies as have pure white petals. Those wilted with age will never do!"

"Yes, Aunt," said Elijah. The simple act of involving him in her activities made him feel useful. Whether picking flowers, milking the cow, or arranging porch furniture, Aunt Winifred appreciated his help and sought his opinion.

She followed him to a nearby patch. "What is thy feeling about the flowers in this group?" she asked. "Shall we pick them or leave them as seed for next year's crop?" She paused and tilted her head, waiting for Elijah's response.

"I think they look old and past their time," said Elijah. "They'll be good for seeding."

"I agree," said Aunt Winifred, "except thee should not be too critical about age! Why, an old flower will soon be born into a new expression of living, as shall we all. Not a bad thing, thinks thee?"

Elijah didn't like it when his great aunt spoke this way. It made him feel she was talking about herself, aging, thinking about death. But, ironically, death was on his mind today, too.

"Oh, Aunt, I only meant the flower was not as bright as the rest."

"I know, dear one, I know," she said, inclining her head and smiling.

"Aunt, I am having dreams again, and they are frightening me."

"Ah, still the dreams," Aunt Winifred said, as if to herself. "So, the gift is revealed in another...surely now the gift, and not just random dreams thee has."

"Another came last night," Elijah said.

"What do they show thee?"

"They are dreams of sadness, Aunt—dreams of dying. The Union is gone, the meetinghouse, all replaced by open fields and broken foundations."

"This vision is God's gift to you, Elijah, as it was to your father's cousin Joseph. You must acknowledge it, seek to deepen into it. In time the meaning will come clear."

Elijah thought of his struggles in the meeting to focus on the Light. The dreams seemed to push him farther away. How could they be a sign of it? "But Aunt," he asked. "How can I do this? I try to keep in the quiet, I try to be silent and seeking, but my mind is busy. I shall never find the peace my father and brothers do."

"Oh, stop this nonsense," she replied, continuing to grip her daisy-filled apron. "Elijah, dear one, the Light has sought thee, found thee…it is grace…God's gift…the dreams are thy special way to the Light. Thee must not deny this gift, but be silent in awe before it. God knows the language of thy silent soul. Thinkest thee is the only one with this gift?"

Elijah remembered how, long ago, Aunt Winifred told him she had Cousin Joseph's gift as well. He knew she would tell him about it once more.

"Elijah, I have a dream that comes again and again," said Aunt Winifred, closing her eyes, reciting the story as if for the first time. "In my dream I see the great Lombardy poplars behind the meetinghouse, standing tall and strong against the blue sky. Their leaves crackle with the wind, like the wind of God's spirit itself, breathing life into our Union, life into us all. But there is a disruption in my dream, and suddenly I view the rotted stumps of those beautiful trees. The meetinghouse is in ruins, and the cemetery is full, the field populated by scores of plain white stones. The Friends are gone in my dream, Elijah…the Friends will be gone, I fear, when those trees stand no more."

"But how can we stop this from happening, Aunt?"

"Keep in the Light, Elijah. The way of the world and its people may try to lure thee away, but thee must be an example, and let thy Light shine for them. Stay in the Light, Elijah. Believe that Truth lies there. Soon I shall go fully to the Light of God, so it shall remain for thee and thy generation to seek power for thy soul—by uniting with the changeless God."

"But I cannot find the Light as others do," protested Elijah, thinking about his father's constant correction and instruction before and after meeting.

"And that alone is the Truth, dear one," said Aunt Winifred. "For each must find his way to the Light, in company with, but separate from the others." She reached into her apron and pulled out a single perfect daisy. "Like the petals of this flower, we connect to the bright yellow of God's Light, each independent of the other. The nearer we come to the Light, the nearer we come to each other, like the spokes of a wagon's wheel, in true Unity. Why dost thee think I love this flower so? No one can connect thee to God, Elijah. God has found thee and holds thee close even now. Open thy heart's eye and see."

"My father seems to know the way I should seek," Elijah offered.

"Thy father is little able to dictate thy ways. I fear he, like so many others, has only rules and regulations. His life's energy should be spent living as an example, not as a judge of others, especially you, dear one." Elijah smiled at his great aunt's unfailing support of him.

"But Aunt—will my dreams ever show me a happy future?"

"Trust they will, dear one—in time."

Elijah remembered the other reason he'd come this way to Goshen. "Has thee heard of the invasion, Aunt?" Elijah asked.

"Only yesterday my sister's son rode to tell me of the happenings. On first day, thousands of British marched past her home in Chazy. When she asked what they were about, one in a tattered red coat shouted, 'We're off to capture Plattsburgh.' She closed her door in fear, though some neighbors shouted insults at them. A small group of local men tried to slow them, but they continued coming our way."

"Does thee think they will come here, to the Union?" Elijah asked, feeling emptiness in his stomach.

"How can we know what will happen in time of war? Our lot is to keep apart, to seek the Light of peace and understanding. At fifth day meeting we must pray for wisdom to cope with this time, but we must avoid the conflict. We should help those who seek us out for safe harbor, but we must preserve our way of life."

Elijah was about to ask what they might do if British soldiers did invade their peaceable home, but his question was interrupted by the steady hoof beats of a galloping horse. Elijah looked south and saw Jamie Green approaching at great speed. He slowed his horse and trotted up to the rail where Elijah had tied Esther and Ruth.

"Hello, Elijah," Jamie Green said, grinning. "And good day to you, too, Aunt." Elijah smiled hearing his friend call Aunt Winifred "Aunt," a term of respect and not of family relationship.

"Hello, Jamie," said Elijah. "What brings thee here so fast?"

"I have news of the invasion, Elijah, from the men at the inn! I was on errands for my father and heard their talk. All the local men of the militia have been called out. The British are on the Beekmantown Road. There may be fighting! Today! Word is even boys our age are trying to sign up!"

Elijah felt short of breath. A cold chill made him silently shudder. He glanced north up the road, half expecting to see a line of red marching their way. "I must get to Goshen and leave this corn so I might return home," he said, not able to conceal the tremor in his voice.

"That's why I came to find thee," Jamie said. "When I went to thy farm to tell thee and learned thee were on the way to Keese's Mill, I knew I must come. Together we'll learn all there is to learn about the invasion from John Keese, or so says my father."

Elijah had to agree. Though he was a Friend, and one of the first settlers in the region, John Keese still kept his ears open for news about world's people and their affairs. He took great delight in pointing out their flaws and foibles, but didn't hesitate to do business with them. He knew everyone at Goshen and in Peru Village. He would surely have detailed information. Still, Elijah felt frightened. "Let's just go home," he said. "This corn can wait for a safer day to travel," he said, realizing he would be postponing his talk with John Keese about the apprenticeship.

"Don't be afraid, Elijah," said Jamie. "The British are miles from us, keeping along the lakeshore, so they say. They'll not come so close to the mountains."

Reluctantly, Elijah untied Esther and Ruth, turning them toward the road. He climbed on the seat, and Jamie clambered up after him. "Aunt, might I leave my horse under thy care?" called Jamie.

"I shall watch thy horse, and hope for thy safe return," Aunt Winifred answered. "Please come back this way that I might know thee both are safe."

"Come on, Elijah!" Jamie yelled, slapping Elijah on the shoulder. "An adventure awaits like none we've ever had!"

Elijah grunted and snapped the reins. Suddenly he was in no hurry to get to Goshen's Mill.

CHAPTER SIX

The waterwheel on John Keese's gristmill turned slowly counterclockwise, lifted by the flow of the Little Sable River at Goshen. To Elijah, the turning wheel indicated the miller was at work inside. He hoped Jamie's presence and news of the pending invasion wouldn't interfere with his main intent: to discuss the miller's apprenticeship. He was not sure what was causing his stomach to flutter—the danger of an invading force of British soldiers or the thought of discussing plans without his father's knowledge.

The steady swish of the wheel, the splash of water, were drowned out by a low rumble as the boys pulled the thick timbered door and entered the old stone millhouse. They climbed a short series of steps to a heavily reinforced plank floor above the level of the river. Just below the floor, gears and belt-driven disks turned by the great wheel transferred the river's force to a shaft upon which was attached a heavy, grooved stone. This stone was suspended, spinning, above a stationary stone, similarly grooved.

Higher up on a wooden platform stood John Keese,

pouring grist by the measured scoop into the hopper. The grain fell through an opening in the stone and was pulverized into powder. Below, his brother Stephen held a sack at the metal output chest, collecting the whole-grain flour. The scraping of the millstone coupled with the deep rumble of the geared mechanism below sent chills up Elijah's spine. Jamie wrinkled his nose at the overpowering aroma of ground grain, a sweet nuttiness, but Elijah inhaled deeply. The smell shook him out of his nervousness. For a moment he forgot about invading armies and a disapproving father.

John Keese, a short, stocky man, reminded Elijah of a tree stump. His bald head was topped by a smallish hat, while his long, white apron attempted to protect the linsey-woolsey trousers and loose-fitting, collarless, beige shirt, fastened with loops and rolled up to the elbow. In spite of the apron, his clothing was spotted with grain. A perpetual half smile made John Keese appear as if he had just heard a funny story or was about to tell one.

He looked up from the hopper. Behind him were several sacks of grain, the miller's toll for the day's work. John Keese grinned at the boys. His brother, Stephen, known for being a man of few words, nodded his greeting. Most people said John Keese did the talking while Stephen did the rest.

"I need a breather, young fellows," shouted John Keese over the noise of the machinery. "Would either of thee care to give a try at the hopper? My crooked old back could use some straightening."

"No, thank thee," yelled Jamie. "That twirling thing scares the life out of me. I can imagine my hand getting caught in there."

"I'll try," said Elijah, scrambling up the stairs to the platform above the spinning millstone.

"Just pour the wheat into the hopper and let the auger draw it down. The river, the wheel, and the stones do the rest."

Elijah watched as the buds and crowns of wheat cascaded into the hopper, fed toward the millstone by the auger. The air was redolent with the aroma of crushed wheat, and he marveled how the golden wheat, as if by magic, emerged as flour below.

"It's a sort of miracle in my mind," said John Keese. "I never tire of watching the transformation." It was just what Elijah had been thinking.

As Elijah emptied the last of the grain into the hopper, John Keese crossed the mill and waited until the pulverized grain stopped falling into the receptacle below the stone. He pulled hard on a wooden lever, the clutch that would stop the sixteen-foot water wheel from turning. The crash of the thrown lever plunged the mill into silence. The only sound was the gentle flow of the river outside.

"Well, now, boys, why have I the honor of thy company on this beautiful day?" John Keese asked. Stephen Keese began scooping flour into sacks as John gestured for Jamie and Elijah to come further into the mill.

"We bring some of last season's corn for milling," said Elijah. "So great was our harvest we still had much stored in the east barn."

"I'll take my toll and start straight off," said John Keese. "These stones have been rarely still these last weeks. Never have we had such work, it seems, since Stephen there and I brought the stones from Duchess County in '05. Have thee heard the story of that trip?" John Keese asked. Elijah nodded. He had heard the story—many times—each time with a new twist.

"Yes, I'm sure I've told thee the story before," said John Keese, "but perhaps young Green here hasn't heard it."

"I have not heard, it's true, Master Keese, but if you please, I would like to hear instead about the coming British," Jamie said.

"It was a hard winter that year," started John Keese, ignoring Jamie's request. "Stephen there and I made our way back to the Settlement of our birth and contracted the purchase of two fine stones, one to serve as the stationary stone, one to spin above. Each was hewn with great care by a master, and the grooves were sharp and beautifully curved."

"How did thee bring the stones back, and why in the winter?" asked Elijah, knowing the answer but not wishing to hear yet about the British.

"We took strong teams and sleighs and, once upon Lake Champlain, the journey was not difficult. The smooth runners make the job a lark for the team, an effortless pull over the ice. Why, we traveled so fast that Stephen there blew off the sleigh and it was several rods before I knew he was gone. He's a quiet one, thee knows." John Keese winked at Elijah and Jamie; Stephen Keese, finished now with packing the flour, merely shook his head and chuckled.

"John Keese, what do thee know of the coming invasion? Is it true thousands of the British are near Beekmantown?" interrupted Jamie. Elijah was surprised at Jamie's persistence. It was not wise to appear impertinent with an adult.

"Aye, thee has heard the truth," answered John Keese. His perpetual smile faded. "They mass at Chambly, word has it, sixteen thousand soldiers. They build ships on the Richilieu. Days ago our army departed for Sackets Harbor with four thousand soldiers, leaving only fifteen hundred at Plattsburgh, mostly the sick. Towns have called out their militias. Our own David Cochran of Peru Village and his men have gone north to Beekmantown. These British scalawags hope to annex us, regain some territory lost in the last war. But we've been free since 1776, and that freedom is God's gift. We must somehow try to support this effort as we can, even if we stay away from the conflict. After all, we have the testimony of peace to which we aspire."

These were strange words for Elijah to hear coming from the mouth of a fellow Friend. It almost seemed John Keese was in favor of fighting, but Elijah couldn't be sure. Perhaps certain times called for the defense of the very gift of God. Perhaps this was such a time.

Elijah felt his stomach jumping again. "Do thee think they will come here?" he asked.

"We cannot know what such a powerful enemy force

will do, or where they will go," John Keese answered. "But judging from the number of Plattsburgh's citizens passing by on the way to friends and relatives in Peru, I'd judge this place will see no violence. But Plattsburgh, 'tis almost certain, will be the scene of a great siege. If this enemy is not stopped, this land we inhabit will be assimilated into Canada." He smiled sadly and shook his head. "I'll never understand why men decide the only way to settle a dispute is by war."

"We should do more than seek shelter here in Peru!" said Jamie. "What if we wish to do our part to preserve our freedom? Men in the Union have heard how boys are trying to join units to fight. What of that?"

"Martin Aikin of Essex passed through here in the last days of eighth month, on his way to Plattsburgh," said John Keese. "He was gathering provisions to take north and stopped here and at the Yellow Store. He spoke of joining a rifle unit. He's headstrong and independent, perhaps nineteen or thereabouts, known to my family since his youth. Some men of our militia have already come home, finding the nearness of conflict too much to bear, and have told the story of how Aikin has formed a rifle company of boys like thee, too young to serve in the militia or army."

"I should like to know more about them," said Jamie. "I should like to meet them, and have a word with them."

"Thee may not get that chance," said John Keese. "Aikin's Company has gone north, we hear, to help form the line of defense near Beekmantown. It is possible they could be killed there."

Elijah's nervous stomach made him change the subject. "Excuse me, John Keese, but my brother, Israel, tells me thee would like to speak with my father about something."

"Yes, I plan another mill downriver at Peru Village. Stephen will be the master miller at that location. Thy father is a good man of business. I'm seeking his opinion on this expansion."

"Will the invasion change thy plan?" asked Elijah, downcast since it seemed John Keese only wanted his father's business advice.

"My boy, we Friends sometimes find our lives overcome by forces we cannot control, but our hope is these English have more important destinations and will leave us alone once they acquire what they seek."

Elijah considered this. "And what of the new mill then?"

"I will proceed as I have planned. I am in search of an apprentice who would like start with me at the end of ninth month. He will have lodging and meals with my family and will accompany Stephen and myself to Duchess County this winter as we procure a millstone for the new mill. It is quite an adventure, and we could use youthful assistance. We are not as young as once we were!" His smile returned. "And some local lad might spend the winter without the smell of the barn on him."

"When my brother, Israel, told me he had spoken with thee, I thought thee wished to speak to my father about an apprenticeship," Elijah said, before he could stop himself.

"Oh, thy father is too old to be my apprentice!" said John Keese, his eyes twinkling. Stephen looked up from his work and laughed at the joke.

Elijah felt his face grow warm. Perhaps his dream of apprenticeship was just that...a dream, and a foolish one at that.

"And, yes, Israel, thy brother," said John Keese, his smile widening. "Does that young man still work the farm? I see him about town quite frequently."

"He has been often in town to make deliveries," said Elijah. Elijah wondered why John Keese should have such a sudden interest in Israel's whereabouts.

"'Tis not the deliveries here I refer to," John Keese said, winking at Stephen. "The lad has been observed spending time at Elmore's Store, and on the streets of town. And it might be said the lad's not lonely. Someone shares the buckboard seat aside him."

Elijah did not understand. Israel's trips to town were about business for the farm. What else could John Keese be talking about? "I only know my father directs my brother's duties when coming to town," said Elijah. "He expects Israel to complete his task and return to work at home."

"Whatever thee thinks," said John Keese, clapping Elijah on the shoulder. "Tell thy father I wish to speak to him. In the meantime, I have flour and meal to deliver to Elmore's. On thy way home, can thee take it there for me?"

Elijah considered the extra mile out of his way and

how his father would be awaiting his return. "Yes, I can do that for thee," he answered with reluctance. Becoming an apprentice had excited him. To be a delivery boy was embarrassing.

"It will not take us long, Elijah," added Jamie. "Come, I'll help thee load."

Goshen and Peru Village were linked by a dusty, well-traveled road, only a mile distant from one another along the river. Jamie chattered about the coming invasion. Elijah was lost in thought. Did John Keese want him or not? Why else would the miller need to speak to his father? But Ben Hoag would not respond to questions of business from John Keese. Ben had more than once implied that some of the Keeses had Hicksite leanings. And what could the miller have meant about Israel being about the streets of town? Farm business brought Israel to town, although lately he had seemed more than willing to come whenever the opportunity arose.

"Ahead be Elmore's," noted Jamie as they approached the two-story brick edifice. The storekeeper stood on the wide front porch, a tall, slender man wearing a long, white apron, holding a broom. Several locals sat in assorted chairs on the porch, deep in conversation. The boys pulled up to the rail and trough. Asa Elmore leaned on his broom and smiled, his wide mustache upturned.

"Good morning, lads," he called, his eyes crinkling in a friendly way. "What brings two of the Union's finest out on such a bright morning?" The men on the porch stopped their conversation and turned their attention to the boys.

"If it please thee, we bring a delivery from John Keese at the mill in Goshen," said Elijah. Jamie slid off the wagon seat and prepared to start unloading the ground grain on the loading platform.

"That John Keese! I've been after him for a week now about a delivery. It's high time he makes good on his promise to send me something to sell. This war has everything in short supply, what with trying to feed an army. Townspeople need to eat, too."

Jamie struggled to get a grip on a sack of flour, and Elijah went around to help. "Leave it for us, boys," Mr. Elmore said. "Harry," he yelled to a sleepy-eyed lad of about fifteen slouched on the bench outside the big double door. "Get off your duff and lend a hand here!"

Harry groaned and eased himself to his feet, stretched, and shuffled down the stairs.

"Have to keep a fire lit under that boy all the time," Asa Elmore said, but then added, with a grin, "but that's all going to change soon, I'd expect." He swatted Elijah on the shoulder and winked. "I'm surprised to see you, young Hoag. What's become of your elder brother?"

"Israel is at home at work," answered Elijah, uncomfortable with Asa Elmore's tone of familiarity. What did he care about Israel?

"Your Pa finally getting a last bit of work out of him then, before the Methodist-Episcopal church gains a new convert?" He smiled as though he and Elijah shared a secret. The men on the porch all chuckled and made comment, too low for Elijah to hear.

"I don't know what you mean," Elijah said.

Asa Elmore continued to smile his friendly smile. "Yes, I can see you don't, but you will soon enough, I'll wager. He seems a fine young man, that brother of yours."

"Yes, he is," responded Elijah, now thoroughly confused about the direction the conversation had taken. All he wanted now was to get on his way. Harry had finished loading a pull cart and was struggling to tug it up a narrow ramp that connected loading platform to porch. "Come, Jamie, we are late enough," Elijah said.

"The Peru militia," blurted Jamie, "has it left for battle?"

"Aye, lad, it has. Today may be the day they engage the enemy, near Beekmantown. They've made a stand, but shan't do much against the onslaught, I'd say. God help David Cochran. God help us all."

Elijah encouraged Esther and Ruth's noses out of the water trough, aiming them south toward the rickety wooden bridge that spanned the little Sable at Peru Village. Up in the seat, he turned to Asa Elmore, who had begun to push the cart from behind to ease Harry's struggle. They reached the porch and Mr. Elmore stood, stretching his back.

"Good day, then," Elijah called.

"Good day to you, boys. Give my best to John Keese when next you see him. And give my best, too, to your brother." He turned to Harry, now slouched in his place on the bench. "Land sakes, boy," he shouted, as Elijah and Jamie drove down the sloped roadway toward the bridge, "I can't sell merchandise from the front porch! Move it to the storeroom!"

Elijah guided the horses across the narrow passage over the bridge. Below, to his left, the water-driven businesses on the Little Sable—the grist and sawmills, plus other buildings—made up the industrial heart of the town; to his right, a mill pond, created by the dam beneath, was covered by a blanket of logs, awaiting the sawmill. On its surface floated enough timber to build many houses. He could hear the whine of saws midway across the river. The smell of sawdust pervaded the air. It was a good smell, a smell of progress. The horses pulled up the rise with ease and followed the bend in the road, the Union road. Elijah was taking the main route home. It was faster, and he wanted to get there. He couldn't shake the growing fear of red-coated soldiers on the outskirts of town.

"Exciting, isn't it?" Jamie broke into his thoughts. "To have the war so close to us! I want to learn of it, Elijah. I am feeling that I want to get closer to it."

"But fighting a war, fighting of any kind, is against our belief," Elijah said. "It is one thing to support war in words, from a distance, but to take up arms to kill a man?" Elijah thought of John Keese and his Aunt Winifred; although neither of them would fight, neither stated their opposition to resisting the invasion.

"It seems to sharpen the meaning of life for me, Elijah. I don't see myself sitting in meeting all my days, avoiding the world that waits outside, like some butterfly safe in a cocoon. Besides, I have trouble seeing my future. I don't think I'm destined to live a long life," Jamie said.

"Don't say that," Elijah said. "Thee cannot predict what will come." Elijah thought of Cousin Joseph and his visions, of his Aunt Winifred and her dreams of the Lombardy poplars, of his own troubling nightmares of death and the end of the Union. "No one can predict future time," he said, doubting his own words.

"I mean it," said Jamie quietly. "I believe I will die young. The war may be my destiny. I need to speak to Martin Aikin and the boys who follow him."

A wagon approached from the south, a horse-driven buggy with a lone driver. As it neared, Elijah recognized Israel. Why would Israel be heading toward town now? Was he looking for him? As they passed, Israel quickly glanced at his brother and nodded, but made no attempt to slow or speak. "Where are thee going?" called Elijah. But Israel continued on his way, the buggy wheels throwing a spray of dirt.

"An errand for thy father, perhaps?" Jamie offered.

"Not at midday. I fear something is wrong," said Elijah. "We must get home. We'll take the back road. We've yet to retrieve thy horse." Elijah had the uncomfortable feeling that his nightmare might yet come true.

CHAPTER SEVEN

Fourth Day, September 7, 1814

Seventh hour in the morning, and Elijah was still angry from the previous day. No trouble at home. No danger. And no Israel either. He and Jeremiah had labored all afternoon in the wheat field, baked dry by the sun. Elijah had struggled with the cradle, dumping the sheared wheat in disheveled piles. Once again, at his father's direction, he switched jobs with Jeremiah and, with rake in hand, followed his father and younger brother as they cut the wheat in wide swathes, laying it gently on the ground. Elijah combined nearby piles and tied them into shocks.

The heat of the day did not exceed the heat of Elijah's anger and frustration over his missing brother. His father's silence and assumed acceptance of Israel's absence aggravated him even more. They completed barn chores and still their older brother was absent. "He's nineteen now, and bound to be on business of his own," offered Ben Hoag. But the faraway look in Ben's eyes told Elijah his father was as confused as they about Israel's whereabouts.

Long past dark last night Elijah had lain awake,

listening for his brother's arrival, which had not come before he drifted into exhausted sleep. Now, his arms and shoulders stiff, his hands openly blistered from the field work, Elijah feared they were starting another day of the same—acres of wheat to harvest without the aid of the strongest, most efficient son, the one who could easily do the work of two. Elijah had had enough. Today Israel must be told. And if his father would say nothing, he would. All Israel needed to do was come to work.

"Milking is done, Elijah," said Jeremiah. "Pa is finishing with the horses while I feed the chickens. Will thee help me afterward with the steers?"

"Of course," fumed Elijah, "though that job might be accomplished by Israel, if he were here."

"Remember to close the gate," said Jeremiah.

"Do thee think I would make the same stupid blunder twice in two days?" Elijah snapped, immediately seeing the hurt look in his younger brother's eyes. He took a deep breathe and exhaled. "But thank thee, Jeremiah, for reminding me."

"I was only trying to help," said Jeremiah, picking up a bucket of grain for the chickens. "I will see thee at breakfast," he said.

As Jeremiah exited the small side door, the large sliding door at the end of the barn opened. Israel latched the door open and stepped inside.

"Elijah," he called down the length of the barn, "since thee have nothing to do I can use thee to help with the steers." He started up the center alley toward Elijah.

Elijah felt his anger forming the words before he spoke them. "Israel Hoag, I do the work of this farm at our father's bidding, not yours. It seems thee has forgotten thy own place among us!"

"I have had business about town that has kept me away," said Israel, drawing near.

"Business?" shouted Elijah. "And what business keeps thee away until well past nightfall and is more important than carrying thy weight, doing thy share of the work? Are thee no longer our brother? Jeremiah and I alone have done barn chores and field chores while thee ride about the streets of Goshen and Peru Village. And thee nearly ran me off into a field in thy haste to go to the village on third day. Are thee one of us or not?"

Israel, usually calm and peaceable like their father, bristled, his face red. "Watch thy words, Elijah. Thee forgets thy place in this family."

"At least I am still a part of the family," said Elijah. "It would seem thee are trying to give up thy place. Thee has certainly given up the work."

Israel reached out a ham-sized fist and snatched Elijah by the front of his shirt, lifting him easily off the floor. Elijah's arms dangled behind him like a doll's. He was so angry he had momentarily forgotten just how strong his brother was. Now he remembered.

Israel glared at Elijah through bloodshot, weary eyes. His grip tightened as he drew Elijah's face closer to his. Elijah was beginning to gasp for breath.

"Does thee know what it means to be disowned, Elijah?" Israel said through clenched teeth.

Elijah knew. To be disowned was to be removed from the Fellowship, no longer able to attend meeting, no longer able to call oneself a Friend. "Are thee to be disowned for not doing thy work?" Elijah gasped.

Israel let go of Elijah's shirt, and Elijah fell back against a post, sliding to a sitting position on a bale of straw. His shirt was rumpled and damp from the sweat of his brother's hand. He looked up at Israel, now breathing hard, but seemingly calmer. Elijah had never in fourteen years seen his brother so distressed. "Why do thee speak of disownment?" asked Elijah, hoping the question wouldn't provoke any more anger. He was grateful to have survived thus far.

"I have fallen in love with a girl from the village. She is not from among the Friends," began Israel. "I cannot live here any more apart from her. I have asked her to marry me and have asked her father's permission, which he has granted. I will move into the village to begin a life there with her."

Elijah jumped to his feet and leaned toward Israel, his fists clenched.

"Leave?" Elijah fairly shouted, but then caught himself. "How will thee support thyself apart from this farm?" he continued in a loud whisper.

"Martha's father is Asa Elmore, who owns the general store. He will employ me."

Elijah felt as though he had been struck in the back of the head. Israel's distant attitude, his frequent absences from the farm, Asa Elmore's behavior—suddenly it all came clear.

"But what will Pa say?" said Elijah.

"Our father will say what he must. He will see to it that I am visited by members of the meeting. They will try to talk me out of this. They will tell me to say I am sorry. But it is too late. My decision is made. I will tell Pa when I feel the time is right, but not yet. And thee are to say nothing of what has passed between us." Israel turned and strode out of the barn.

Before Elijah could make any sense of what had just happened, Sarah Green walked through the open side door. Sarah Green…before eighth hour in the morning! "Good morning to thee, Elijah," Sarah said. "Did thy brother not tell thee I was here?"

"My brother and I discussed other things," Elijah said. He smoothed the front of his shirt, still rumpled from Israel's fist. His face felt warm, and his heart pounded at seeing her. Sarah, who was dressed for barn chores in heavy cloth pants, work shirt, and boots, of all things, certainly didn't appear to be a young lady. But at a busy season like the harvest, with only her father and Jamie to run their farm, it made sense Sarah would need to help. Their mother could handle the housework.

"My father sent me to borrow some straw for bedding in the barn. Our supply has run out. Thy brother Israel was to give me some. My wagon is just outside."

"Ours is in the east barn," said Elijah. "Come." Elijah grasped a pitchfork leaning against a post. The sun was higher in the sky now, and he squinted toward it. "Drive below the loft door and I'll load."

The previous year's wheat harvest had yielded more

than an ample amount of straw, and the loft of the east barn still bulged with the shocks. Elijah pushed the wooden loft door open, forked a shock, and pushed it out the door. It fell to the wagon, bits of straw flying in the air. Sarah coughed, then giggled, brushing the bits of straw from her clothing. "I need only the straw, Elijah. Thee may keep the dust!"

Elijah smiled. If Rebecca had spoken those words, he might have taken offense. But Sarah's tone was light and airy, and her eyes crinkled in a friendly way. "Stand away," he said. "I'll send some others to thee." He pushed three more shocks out the door and each showered the air with debris. Sarah watched from below, hands on her hips.

"Our thanks to thee, Elijah," Sarah said, climbing into the wagon seat. "I must get this home."

"Has thee a need to see Rebecca?" Elijah asked, wishing she would stay longer. "She's at the house preparing breakfast. Thee might stay and have the meal with us."

"Oh no, I must get back. Father told me not to dawdle here. He knows me too well," she said, laughing.

"Elijah!" boomed a voice. Elijah was so startled he nearly fell out of the door. Ben Hoag's bulk seemed to fill the loft. "What are thee doing now?"

"Pa! I…uh…," he stammered. "I was giving straw to Sarah Green. Israel gave her leave to borrow some of ours. Their supply is short, it seems, and I…"

"Short supply, eh?" growled Ben Hoag. "Perhaps the Greens would have an ample amount if Samuel Green were not so intent on selling everything he owns to feed the King's army." He tromped to the loft door and looked down on Sarah. "What of that, young Sarah Green? Has thy father no shame to borrow my straw because he has sold his off? And how I am to know the straw I loan thee is for thy barn? Perhaps thy father has some other plan for it?"

Sarah looked up at Ben Hoag, leaning out the door, nearly crushing Elijah against the frame. "I know not, Ben Hoag; I only know what my father asked of me this day—to ask your kindness in the loan of straw for our animals." She met his angry gaze with her brown eyes opened wide, unblinking. Her quiet, measured tone seemed to calm Ben. Elijah felt his father shift back out of the doorway. Elijah could stand straight again, and breathe.

"What's done is done," muttered Ben, as he turned to descend the loft stair. "But let this be the end of our dealings with the Greens, and let it be for thee a warning, Elijah. Thee are to spend thy time in work and not in conversation with those who would lead thee astray." He turned to look down at Sarah. "Get ye home," he said. "And tell thy father of our exchange."

Without a word, Sarah snapped the reins, and the old horse pulled away from the East barn. Elijah's stomach lurched. He wanted to say more to Sarah but he would not get the chance. As she clattered down the drive, she looked back and waved. He returned the wave. At least she bore him no ill will.

Standing in the silent loft, Elijah surveyed the

sweeping view of the property—the barns, the outbuildings, the fields—and thought of the constant, exhausting work, one job ending and another beginning, season after season. He watched as Sarah made her way up the Rogers Road toward her family's farm. The soft thud of her horse's hooves gradually faded. Elijah envisioned Sarah and Jamie and their father working the land together. It must be a struggle for the three of them, with Sarah busy inside their house as well.

But if Israel left their farm, life would suddenly be different for the Hoags. Without Israel's strong presence, the role of eldest son, with all the work and responsibilities it entailed, would fall to him. And what of John Keese? What if he intended for Elijah to become his apprentice? What would Ben Hoag say when he learned both his older sons were preparing to leave the farm? Worse, what if no offer came from John Keese? What if the only thing Elijah became in this new arrangement was eldest son?

Elijah stared out the loft door. Sarah's wagon was distant now, the horse's feet moving soundlessly. She was beginning her day's work, and Elijah was facing his. The fields were waiting, as they would be the next day, and the next. He closed the door, latched it, and stood a moment in the warm darkness. He felt momentarily safe there, the loft illuminated only by cracks of light through the boards, shielded from the world of work below. Mounds of straw swallowed up sound, and Elijah heard the silence. How long could he stay here and not be found?

But his feelings of safety gave way to another feeling, of being trapped in a smothering cocoon, a cocoon from which he might not be able to escape. The sweet smell of straw lost its appeal, becoming dusty and oppressive. The straw piles hovered over him like so many boulders, ready to topple. It was hard to breathe. He had to get out, get away. Elijah kicked through the strands of straw on the floor and clambered down the creaking stairs.

Once on the main floor, he burst outside. The air was a wall of fresh coolness, the morning bright with sunshine. Dew sparkled on the grass and fields. The pungent aroma of wood smoke from the kitchen fire drifted across the yard. How easily the world could change by simply walking through a door! Elijah contemplated this notion as he walked up the back steps to breakfast.

CHAPTER EIGHT

Fifth Day, September 8, 1814

Gray, low-hanging clouds and misty rain usually depressed Elijah, but not today. The Hoags' and Greens' fields were soggy and unworkable, so Elijah, Jamie, and Jeremiah were headed toward Goshen. A load of newly harvested wheat filled the wagon, bound for the Yellow Store. In trade for the wheat, Ben Hoag would obtain staple items that could not be produced on the farm—sugar and molasses—to store for the coming winter. Israel had been absent for most of yesterday's field work, so Elijah and Jeremiah had carried his load. Elijah's entire body ached, and even Jeremiah, who thrived on the hard labor, had dark circles under his eyes and had climbed on the wagon that morning with a groan.

Though Elijah looked forward to this day of rest from toil, he had been troubled since Israel's confession. Plus, this was fifth day. They must attend meeting after breakfast. "Thy trip must be quick and efficient," warned Ben Hoag before they left. "Thee need not stop to visit John Keese. Take the wheat to the store, trade it, and come home." And Ben's final words still rang in

Elijah's ears: "Be back in time to go to meeting, Elijah. No one has need of it more than thee."

As they crossed the bridge into Goshen, a crowd of men were gathered on the steps of the Yellow Store. On the porch stood a tall man wearing a light gray suit and broad-brimmed hat. At first glance, he appeared to be a Friend, but then Elijah recognized he was David Cochran, captain of the Peru militia. He would know about the state of the invasion, first hand!

David Cochran was speaking to the men. His eyes looked tired, as though he had slept little or not at all. He glanced up as the boys approached, but continued to address the men.

"It was a horror like nothing I've experienced," he said. "We were outnumbered ten to one." His voice was steady, but soft.

"How did they come?" one man asked.

"They came in two columns," Cochran answered, "one down the Beekmantown Road and another through the cedar swamps along the Lake Road. We, that is, Major John Wool, his regulars, and seven hundred of us militia, exchanged fire on the Beekmantown Road at dawn, then retreated back to Culver's Hill to make a stand. Hundreds of the militia kept running south, headed home. That first volley was all they could stand—they'd had enough, and I can't say I blame them."

"What then?" asked another voice.

"They came at us like water down a ravine, pouring out of the woods into the clearing, marching in rows down the road, coming out of everywhere. We hid behind trees, stone walls—anything we could find—and opened up on them. Our militia fired the first shots. Their front lines collapsed as they took the balls, dead as they struck the ground. One of their officers went down in the opening volleys, and I thought it might slow them, but they swarmed us like bees, as if nothing had happened. They closed ranks, and we saw a line of red charging us, bayonets affixed…and thousands behind them. My God, there's no stopping an onslaught like that."

"What did you do then?" asked the first man.

"Why, we ran like the devil. I'm ashamed to admit we made no long engagement there, but they overwhelmed us. The noise! Shouting and screaming, bodies falling, the hideous smoke so thick you couldn't see to shoot, the red blur racing at us—say nothing of the blood. I cannot shake the sight and sound of it from my memory. Thank Providence for trees to hide behind and rocks to block their fire."

"How did you get away, and what about the other British invaders?" asked the second man.

"We crossed the Saranac above Winchel's mill, then tore up the bridge flooring to use as breastworks to hold them back," Cochran answered. "Col. Appling and his units did the same when his intelligence reported that the enemy had beaten their way through the swamps and were marching on a direct path to Plattsburgh. Even trees the militia have been cutting to block the roadways couldn't deter them. Our gunboats out on the lake fired toward their vanguard at MacDonough's command.

They were hurt, no doubt, but they advanced to the riverbank."

"Is there firing on the village of Plattsburgh yet?" someone shouted out.

"They fired on us all day the sixth and seventh," said David Cochran. "We returned fire on the homes the British occupied as headquarters. We used hot shot and burned the places to the ground. The British responded with more hot shot, burning houses, stores, the courthouse, a jail—all destroyed to give British sharpshooters a clear shot at our battlements."

Elijah listened, his stomach in a knot. So, it was happening. The invasion had begun. He wondered how long before the British army would come here, bringing death and destruction with them. Memory showed him the scene in his dream—the Union gone, perhaps destroyed by the fire of enemy guns.

Jamie, leaning forward, seemed to hang on every word. His eyes flashed, and he stood on the wagon seat. "Excuse me," he called, "but were any boys in the fight?" His voice trembled.

David Cochran looked first at Jamie and then at Elijah before answering. "Aye, lad, there were a group of boys about your age, a dozen or so, who joined Wool at Culver Hill and retreated south to the village with us. They are attached to no unit, but answer only to Captain Aikin and Lieutenant Flagg. They call themselves 'Aikin's Volunteer Rifle Company'…brave young fellows, not easily frightened, and some of them good shots. Three of them crossed the river to a barn behind

British lines on the night of the sixth and stole rum while the British sentry was napping! They barely made it back alive, covered by their companions on the south side of the Saranac." He laughed out loud. "Even General Mooers, commander of the New York State militia, has noted their usefulness." He gestured at the door of the Yellow Store. "Three of them are inside now, helping to gather supplies needed at the Salmon River Settlement, General Mooers' headquarters."

As if on signal, two boys, one Elijah judged to be sixteen, one younger than that, both carrying guns, exited the store and approached David Cochran. The taller boy, thin-faced and bespectacled, spoke.

"Captain, the storekeeper says they have no wheat. Harvest is beginning, but rain has held things up. He suggested we try Elmore's in the village."

"Asa is in short supply as well, Henry," said Cochran. "Farmers have sent their early cuts directly to the gristmills, garnering it for their own supplies, what with the uncertain future."

"What if we don't find any wheat?" asked the other older boy, heavy-set with flaming red hair. Elijah glanced a moment behind the wagon seat at the pile of bulging sacks of wheat.

"General Mooers has sent to Albany for supplies, Jonathan, but couriers are taking extra care on the roads," answered the Captain. He took off his hat and wiped his forehead with the back of his hand. The air was heavy and wet. His glance fell on Elijah and Jamie, sitting in the wagon. He pointed behind them. "What have you in there this early hour, lads?"

Elijah swallowed hard. "Wheat, bound here for trade. My father expects me to leave it in payment for supplies needed at our farm," Elijah's voice crackled, his hands shook.

"Well, what luck!" said Cochran. "Henry! Jonathan!" Cochran turned to the Aikin's boys, "Give this young fellow a hand unloading his wagon. I'll pay the store-keeper and he can issue the proper credit to the Hoags…you are one of Ben Hoag's, are you not? I've done business with your father. I'm sure he'll see the need. Many of your people support this war even though they may not say so. You Quakers will have your lives disturbed by this invasion as well, especially if it's successful."

"We cannot let them get it, Elijah," whispered Jeremiah. "Pa will not approve."

"I know," said Elijah, "but how I can I stop it?" The sale would provide his family with the goods they needed, true enough, but Ben Hoag would only see how it fed an army. War was forbidden. Supporting people in the cause of war was just as bad. His father would suffer public embarrassment. News of the sale would reach the meeting, and Ben Hoag, the overseer, would have to apologize on Elijah's behalf, ask forgiveness, and promise never to let it happen again. It would be a low moment.

"Elijah—this is the way we can help!" said Jamie. "It's our duty to support freedom, as John Keese said. Just tell thy father the truth. Thee left it at the store and someone purchased it ."

"But what will happen when my father hears who made the purchase?" asked Elijah. "What then? He will say it is my fault!"

"Tell him it was my idea," said Jamie. "It's of no matter. He cares little for my family. Let him think again what a bad influence I am on thee."

Elijah gripped the reins. Part of him wanted to snap them and ride away, but he wasn't sure what Cochran and the others would do. He noted the guns the boys carried. Would they shoot him? This was, after all, war. On the other hand, his father had no confidence in his ability to do things according to direction. How could this be any worse than his other blunders?

"I'll speak to your father at the next opportunity," said David Cochran. "I'm sure he will be pleased to know his wheat nourished men who protect our community."

Jamie nudged him in the side, jumping down from the wagon. "Let's do this, Elijah—come, I'll help thee unload." He slid a sack off the wagon onto the loading platform.

"We'll help," said the taller boy Cochran had called Henry, now at the back of the wagon. "Lend a hand, Jonathan," he said to the red-haired one, as another boy emerged from the doorway of the Yellow Store. "Just in time, Hiram. Help us, will you?"

The three members of Aikin's company joined Jamie and the wagon was empty, the sacks piled high on the platform, before Elijah could get out of his seat.

"Excellent!" called Cochran. "I'll send a man with a wagon to retrieve them and pay the store. Thank you, young Hoag. It is my good fortune you came along today!" But Elijah saw no good in it. He wished he had stayed home.

The crowd was breaking up, the men going about their early morning business. David Cochran mounted a horse. He addressed the three Aikin's Volunteers. "Wish I could see you boys back to the Settlement, but I need to check things at my mill and then get back to the forts in Plattsburgh. Most of our militia is still there, keeping the British on the north side of the Saranac." He smiled. "But you're not strangers to walking these last few days, are you?"

The tall boy pushed his glasses up higher on his nose. "No, Captain. We've walked miles since the third: Plattsburgh up to Chazy, then back to Plattsburgh by way of Dead Creek Bridge to get some fighting guns; north to Beekmantown and Culver Hill and back to the mill along the Saranac in Plattsburgh; south to the forts along the lake, then down the Lake Road to Salmon River Settlement, and now here. We've walked and run most of it."

"Except when someone gives us a ride," said the heavy-set redhead. He eyed Elijah's wagon.

"Say," said the tall boy, the one called Henry. "Would that be possible? Could you and your friends take us to the Salmon River Settlement?" He smiled at Elijah in a friendly way, then turned to his two companions. "Jonathan, Hiram…get your gear. This fellow here might give us a ride to save our aching feet!" They grabbed small, grubby haversacks from along the porch rail and slung them over their shoulders, their rifles in hand. In seconds they slid into the back of the buckboard next to Jeremiah. "Beg pardon," Henry said, bumping to a position behind the wagon seat. "Obliged to you for the ride. Now, what was your name?"

Elijah swallowed hard, trying to recall what he might have said to stop this from happening, but, as usual, he was slow with the words. Jamie would've had the words, but Jamie wanted the boys to come.

"My name is Elijah Hoag. Next to thee is my brother Jeremiah. This is my friend, Jamie Green."

"Pleased to make your acquaintance," Henry said. "Name's Henry Averill, but friends call me Hank. This fellow here is Jonathan Woodward, and there already about to take a nap is Hiram Walworth." He gestured to the third boy, lanky and dark-haired, who Elijah judged to bc about sixteen. Hiram had already slouched against the wagon's rail, his head on his haversack, his hat pulled over his eyes.

"My, this is the life," Hiram said, scratching under one arm. "Wake me when we get to the Settlement, fellers."

"How do you expect to sleep in this wagon, hard as a rock and bumping all the way back to the Settlement?" said Jonathan. "It'd be like trying to sleep on the hard barn floor up at Atwood's, eh Hank?"

"Yeah, ol' Hank here decided that barn floor was just too hard," added Hiram, lifting the brim of his hat. "He decided to go up in the hayloft where he could get a little shuteye. Didn't matter a whit to him the militia was already there, snoring away. 'Course it was kind of dark, you know, being the middle of the night, and Hank has big feet, you'll notice. Wasn't long afore he stepped down on some poor militia man's face. What was it he called you, Hank?" Hiram grinned and pulled his hat back over his eyes.

Hank Averill colored slightly and rolled his eyes. "Let's just get on our way," he muttered. "Do you know the way to Salmon River, Elijah?"

Elijah's stomach was in a knot. Part of him knew going to Salmon River Settlement was wrong. But another part of him was intrigued. Imagine boys only a little older than he caught up with the militia, engaged in this conflict. They seemed nice enough. How wrong would it be to take a side trip to Salmon River? They could follow the Lake Road south to its intersection with Arthur Road and return to the Union. A big circle is all it was.

"I do, but we cannot go until I find a way to get my brother home," he said. He was sure if he took Jeremiah home himself, his father would intervene and not allow them to go on. He would admonish the Aikin's boys and send them on their way. Plus, Elijah would have to explain the sale of the wheat before he was sure he had a good explanation. Surely they could find someone in town to take Jeremiah back to the farm.

"There's no time for that," said Jonathan. "We need to get back to the rest of our company. We'll be bound for the river patrol today, upstream. Remember? General Mooers is afraid the British are seeking a crossing further west to attack us from the rear."

"I'll not leave thee, Elijah," said Jeremiah. "I want to go."

"All this talk is keeping me from my nap," spoke Hiram from under his hat. "Let's be on our way, boys."

Jamie nudged Elijah. "Jeremiah will be safe, Elijah. Thee and I can look after him. Let's go to the Settlement. We can continue up Roger's Road to the Salmon River cutoff. It's only a few miles. Why, these fellows have been doing the distance mostly on foot!" He looked at the boys in the back of the wagon with admiration.

"We'll go," Elijah said. "But there'll be no delays at the Settlement. My father will be upset enough at our absence without our being gone all day." He snapped the reins, and Esther and Ruth set off at a fast clip.

"We'll not regret it, Elijah!" Jamie said, his eyes gleaming. "This will be an adventure like none we've had!" He clapped Elijah on the back. Then, turning to Hank, he said, "Did thee truly step on the faces of militia?"

Hank lowered his eyes, then looked up, his face serious. "That and much more. Jonathan, Hiram, and I will tell you about it on our way.

CHAPTER NINE

Elijah kept his eyes on the road as he listened to the account the Aikin's boys told. Gray clouds hung low over them, a misty rain filled the air. Now and then, a wagon carrying people and possessions would pass, going west toward the Union…more citizens of Plattsburgh leaving in the face of the invasion, no doubt. As they continued north on Rogers Road and approached the cutoff to Salmon River Settlement, Hank told of their exploits since the formation of their company on September third. Jamie was turned completely around on the seat, his attention focused on their passengers. Jeremiah had moved up on the wagon seat between his brother and Jamie. His pale face and wide eyes betrayed his fear, and Elijah knew he had made a mistake agreeing to bring his little brother along. It was wrong for them to come, but now they were well on their way and there was no use turning back. Strangely, Elijah's reservations and fear were nearly equal to his fascination with these three boys.

"How did thee join this fight?" asked Jamie, leaning over the back rest, gripping it so his knuckles were white.

"We've known of the British plan for months. It's been all around town," Hank began. "But a few days ago we were in school and heard some men outside saying there was a buildup of British soldiers north of Champlain, and how Plattsburgh was in their path. They put out a call for local militias to come to the defense, so we jumped out the classroom window to see if we could join up. One sure way to let school out early is to have an invasion, isn't that right, fellows?" Hank turned to his companions, but Jonathan lay flat on the wagon bed, sound asleep, and soft snoring emerged from under Hiram's hat.

"Anyway, we went down to the Printing Office where everyone was gathering," continued Hank. "We were too young to sign up, but we got together a group of us boys and made our own company. Among us was Martin Aikin, and we chose him to be our captain, and Azariah Flagg, our lieutenant. Captain Aikin is nineteen and Lieutenant Flagg is twenty-four, the oldest among us."

"How many are thee?" asked Jamie.

"Oh, about twenty, give or take," said Hank. "Our youngest is Peters. He's fourteen, a few months younger than Jonathan there. The next day, Sunday, we met up and headed to Chazy through Beekmantown. The British had crossed into Champlain, and we heard that's where there'd be action. It was powerful hot that day and it poured at night, so we were soaked when we got to Atwood's in West Chazy."

Elijah felt ashamed. While he had sat in meeting on

first day, these fellows were assembling as a company. While he had harvested crops with his father and brother, they were racing to Chazy to defend the valley. They had done something important, while he had been safe at home, as if nothing were happening in the wider world outside his. "When did thee first have to…to fight?" Elijah asked.

"Well, we thought Monday the fifth would be the day," Hank said. "A spy rode by us as we paraded in front of Atwood's, and we thought sure we would meet the British that morning. We got ourselves into position to wait for them, but they never showed…at least not where we thought they would."

"Where did they go?" Jamie asked, leaning even farther over the wagon seat.

"Turns out they stopped at Atwood's after we'd come back south," said Hank. "So we went south to Culver Hill. General Mooers was there with the militia, and he sent us into the woods to watch the British flank, but we never saw it because the British were stopped eight miles north of Plattsburgh. Then the general sent us to Dead Creek Bridge…that's closer yet to Plattsburgh… to meet up with a Colonel Appling of the US Rifle Corps. He said we could join his unit if we disbanded and followed his company's rules and regulations."

"And thee did not join them?" said Jamie.

"We took a vote and decided we weren't about to take orders from some fellow we didn't even know. Colonel Appling said we should go back to Plattsburgh, to the Armory, and trade in our hunting rifles for real military muskets," Hank said. "They're less for aiming and more for pointing and shooting. Plus, they load faster than most rifles."

"When did the fight begin?" interrupted Jamie.

"Next day," said Hank. "That would be Tuesday the sixth. We'd got word the British were on the march, so we ran as fast as we could back toward Beekmantown. When we got to Judge Bailey's house at Halsey's Corners, we could hear firing, and then here came our militia, running straight at us. Some of them were barefoot. We asked them where they were running, with the fighting going on behind them, and one man, no shoes, no hat, with his face all blackened and his clothes tore up, says, 'When you've fought long as us, you'll be glad to retreat, too!'"

"What happened next?" asked Jamie, climbing over the seat and into the wagon bed. "Listen to this, Elijah!" he said.

"I am listening," said Elijah. A feeling of dread washed over him as he thought of the danger these boys had faced. How could they act so calm?

"Newcomb and Walworth, men who were with Gen. Mooers, were screaming at the militia who were running away, trying to get them back to their positions. We heard later Walworth tried to shoot one of the captains who wouldn't rally his troops," Hank said, "but his gun jammed and wouldn't go off. We looked back where we'd come from and saw men in red coats coming at us. We thought the British had ambushed our flank, but turns out they were New York State Dragoons—

they wear red coats, too,"

"Sure a dangerous color to be wearing on that morning!" said Jamie.

"We got in behind a fence just up from Halsey's house and figured the British would come out of the woods ahead of us, but we were wrong," said Hank. "They came down the lane off to our side. We were straight in their sights."

"Were any of thy company shot?" asked Elijah, now wondering what might happen to them if the British had found their way to Salmon River Settlement.

"No...we ran across the road and took cover behind a fence near Judge Bailey's orchard and fired at them," said Hank, "but it did no good. They still came at us like angry red ants."

"Thee had to run?" asked Jamie.

"Aye, run we did," said Hank, "but not before we drew the British line into range of three cannons General Macomb had placed in the road. Their front line came at us, and the artillery fired three times. We hit them with cannonballs and grape shot. Their line went down like chopped trees. There were body parts flying everywhere. But no sooner did they fall than the men behind closed ranks and kept coming, bayonets flashing," said Hank. "All you could see behind them was red, and then more red. There was no end to their number, and we were but a few hundred. So we ran, all right, back toward Plattsburgh."

Elijah remembered David Cochran's description of this battle. But somehow, coming from the mouths of boys his age, it was even more frightening.

"We was cut off from Wool's division, so we crossed the river above the new bridge at Winchel's Mill and headed for the old stone gristmill on the banks of the Saranac," Hank said. "That put us in a good position to hold the British on the North side of the river."

"And thee has held them so far?" Jamie asked, not trying to conceal the excitement in his voice.

"Yes, but the firing was warm yesterday and the day before, almost constant. All anyone has to do is move along the river bank and he's in some redcoat's sights," said Hank. "Their encampment stretches three, maybe four miles west, upriver. Least that's what our spies tell us."

Elijah struggled to remember how far south from the Saranac River the Salmon River Settlement was. A mile south of Pike's Cantonment was it? Or three miles? He had the chilling feeling he was closer now than ever to real danger. Especially since he could see breaks in the trees ahead and could detect the smell of woodsmoke. Elijah noted two cannons near a makeshift flagpole and suddenly longed to be home safe at the Union.

A little further and he spotted clearings and white tents pitched in rows amid the pines. He was so engrossed in the exploits of Aikin's Volunteers he had lost track of how far they'd come. Rows of men carrying rifles marched up and down in the clearing. Others tended fires, sitting on rocks and stumps. Still more militia men gathered in groups, under trees, seemingly deep in conversation. This was the Salmon River Settlement, encampment of General Mooers and the New York State Militia.

"See over near the big pine?" asked Hank. "That's part of our company."

Elijah urged Ruth and Esther on, stopping them where Hank directed. As the wagon slowed, Jonathan and Hiram awoke, and, rubbing their eyes, jumped down and trotted after Hank to the tree.

"Hey, there, fellows! Where is everyone?" called Hiram.

"Captain Aikin and Lieutenant Flagg and some of the boys have hiked toward Pike's Cantonment to try to spot the British," said a lanky, blond boy in his mid-teens. "They told us to stay here and wait for you. So Freddie, Hazen, James, Ethan, and I have been watching the militia drill, resting our bones. Can't do much in this rain."

"When are they expected back, Bartemus?" asked Hank.

"Oh, before mid-afternoon, I expect," answered Bartemus. "Sooner, if they spot anything. Where'd you find the ride?" he asked, eyeing Elijah, Jamie, and Jeremiah. "Them are fine looking horses."

"We met them at Goshen, near Peru Village," said Hank. "They wanted to help us with a ride here, so's we could rest up a bit. This is Elijah, his brother, Jeremiah, and their friend, Jamie. They're from the Peru Union."

Elijah was aware of Bartemus studying them, looking them up and down. "I thought so, by the cut of their shirts and that wide brimmed hat," he said. "Them people are known for being good stockmen, and they raise some of the finest horses in the valley. Morgan, I'd say. How do, fellers."

"Hello," said Jamie, climbing down from the wagon seat. "I'd be pleased to hear about thy time soldiering."

"Jamie, we need to go. Now! Pa will be looking for us." Elijah glanced at Jeremiah, who only nodded. "Will thee get back on with us…please?"

"If thee be in such a hurry, then go. I'll stay awhile and find my own way home," Jamie said.

"But we're miles from the Union, Jamie," Elijah said, feeling his nervousness taking control.

"If Hank and Hiram and Jonathan could walk all those miles, then so can I," said Jamie. "I want to see about joining up with Captain Aikin and his company."

Elijah tried to think of something to say to convince Jamie to come with them. Words failed him as two men in ill-fitting, torn, dirty uniforms approached, walking straight toward Esther and Ruth.

"Say now, Amos, will you look at these fine mares?" said the first militia man. "I could use a mount like this to ease my aching feet." He shifted his rifle and reached out to stroke Ruth's face. The horse snorted and looked away.

"They look to be Morgans, all right, and well-raised, Thomas." He spit a stream of brown juice that splattered on the sleeve of his coat. "And no one knows horses like Amos Finn." He was a short, unshaven, fat man, too large for his uniform. His shirt was gray with grime and grease.

"Jamie, will thee get on so we can leave?" Elijah implored, unable to control the urgency in his voice.

"Not so fast, young feller," said Amos Finn. "Why, you're about to make a sale of a horse! 'Course I can't pay you right off, but you can trust a member of New York's own militia. Especially in a time of war, such as this." He snatched Esther's bridle, but the horse shook him off.

"Spirited thing, ain't she?" Amos Finn said, with a crooked smile. "Well, there's ways to break a horse down to your will. Like I said, no one knows horses like Amos Finn."

"Let go my horse," Elijah said. Before he realized what he was doing, he jumped down from the seat and approached Amos Finn. Jeremiah followed him. "Get away from her," Elijah said, trying to conceal the tremor in his voice. Here on the ground, Amos Finn looked about three times Elijah's size. Perhaps this was not a good idea.

"Well, now what have we got here?" sneered Finn, leaning in toward Elijah. "Fancy talk from the little man." Elijah was overcome by the stench of sweat and tobacco juice, and what he imagined might be liquor on Amos Finn's breath. "What are you, one of them religious types from Peru Union?"

"Why don't you people stay where you belong? God knows you're all cowards, afraid to fight like men." He reached out with a fat fist and smacked Jeremiah so hard he fell to the ground and sprawled there, his arms covering his head.

"Teach him a lesson, Amos!" shouted Thomas, a rum-induced smile on his reddened face.

"I'll teach the little beggar, all right," said Amos Finn. "I'll teach him what it means to be slapped by the same hand what's protecting him and his freedom." He gripped Elijah by the front of his shirt. "You little, yellow pup. You want to live free, then you'd better be ready to fight for it… maybe die for it!" He raised his hand to strike Elijah, and all Elijah could do was brace himself and close his eyes. His arms hung like heavy poles as he waited for Amos Finn's fist to smack into his face.

Elijah felt impact, but not on his face. Something struck him and knocked him to the ground. He opened his eyes, trying to orient himself. Amos Finn lay nearby with Jamie on top, pinning Finn's shoulders to the ground with his knees. Years of heavy farm work had made Jamie strong, and he held Amos Finn down with a hand gripping his face. "Thee will not strike my friend," Jamie hissed. "I'll not stand for it!"

"Get off me," gagged Finn, but Jamie leaned in, pinning him harder to the ground.

"Help, help us," cried Thomas, eyes wild. "This crazy boy will kill him!" Hank and Hiram each held Thomas by an arm.

A group of militia men at a nearby fire dropped their guns and came, running. Three of them pulled Jamie off Amos Finn, who struggled to his feet, choking and red-faced. One of the men punched Finn in the arm. "Starting fights with boys, eh, Finn?" he chided. "You might better save your strength for fighting British!"

"Looks like he might have some trouble with that," said another. "unless he brings that boy along to help him!" The men of the militia roared with laughter and pushed Amos Finn along ahead of them. Thomas pulled free and followed. Elijah stood, trembling, unable to move. He hadn't been able to lift a finger against the man's attack, and Jamie had taken on the fight for him. He felt relief…and shame.

"Jamie…why?" Elijah said. Would he have fought back if Jamie hadn't intervened? He didn't know.

His friend grinned at him and wiped his forehead with his sleeve. "It was no trouble, Elijah," he said. "I've wanted a fight of my own for a time now. Lucky for me thee brought one to me!"

In the distance, rifle fire crackled, and the sound of running feet crashed through the underbrush. The men who had been lounging under trees and around campfires jumped to their feet. It was as if the whole camp paused to listen, ready to react. Several boys with guns, accompanied by two older, but still-young men, emerged from the woods to the north.

"It's Captain Aikin and Lieutenant Flagg," said Hank, "and our companions in the company! Gus! Ira! Hazen! Over here!"

The group turned and walked over to where Elijah's wagon stood. They carried rifles and had ration bags slung over their shoulders, the same bags that Hank, Jonathan, and Hiram carried. One young man was older than the rest, so Elijah guessed he was Lieutenant

Flagg. The man looked at Hank and said, "Gather the company. We need to head back toward the Saranac. The British are all up and down the river, looking for a crossing. We've fired into the trees on the other side, and they've returned fire. We need to keep it hot to hold them back from the river's edge, or they're likely to find a way. General Macomb fears they're looking to cross somewhere upriver then attack Plattsburgh's flank. Some of our company remained along the banks to hold a position."

"We're all here, Lieutenant Flagg," said Hank, "and some new blood, too." He grinned at Elijah and Jamie. "Here's your chance, fellows. Are you ready to see some action?"

"I am, that's sure," said Jamie, still flushed from his tangle with Amos Finn. "How about it, Elijah? It'll be an adventure like none we've…"

"No, Jamie, no," interrupted Elijah. "I can't stay here anymore. Jeremiah is afraid, and so am I. I've no fight in me. Come. Let's go back home."

"I'm going with them, Elijah, if they'll have me," Jamie said. He walked over to stand by the young volunteers.

"We can always use another man," said Jonathan.

"Can you shoot a gun?" asked Hiram. "You might have to, you know."

"Thee will see that I can shoot," said Jamie. "I hunt for our family's food."

"It's not much different, really," said Hiram. "Just that the target shoots back, is all, so you got to make your first shot count!"

Elijah listened to this talk in amazement. He couldn't understand their casual attitude about killing. How could they be so hardened? His insides were quivering at the thought of being so near to violence. His only thought was to get himself and his brother home safely.

"Let's go then," said Jamie, and turning to Elijah, he added, "Don't worry, my friend. We shall see each other in another day, perhaps two." He paused. "But I think thee should not tell my family where I am."

"I'll not tell," Elijah said. "But I wish thee would come with us."

"I shall, in a day or two," said Jamie, with a smile. "And such stories I'll tell thee!"

He turned with Aikin's Company and started back north along the edge of the trees. Someone handed him a rifle. Jamie turned, smiling, and held it aloft. He pointed to it and pumped his arm as if in a cheer. A quick wave and he was out of sight in the woods.

Elijah stood a long moment and stared after him. The rain intensified, blown by a cool wind. Elijah felt numb, outside and in. Gone were any questions about his involvement in this violence. He had to get away from it. The foul smell of Amos Finn lingered in his nostrils.

"Elijah, can we go home now?" Jeremiah asked. "I'm scared."

"Yes," Elijah answered. It was what he wanted more than ever to do.

They climbed into the wagon, turning Ruth and Esther back the way they came, away from the river, away from the forts, away from the coming conflict. But Elijah couldn't escape the feeling he was replacing one place of trouble for another. At home, his father would be waiting.

CHAPTER TEN

Elijah gripped the reins so hard his knuckles stood out like little white pebbles. All the way back to Peru Village his eyes strained, scrutinizing every rock and tree, half expecting a red-coated soldier to step into his path and take aim. He and Jeremiah spoke little, but Elijah could guess what his brother was thinking. It was late afternoon now, the time just before chores. Their father would be doing odd jobs around the buildings, kept out of the field by the wet conditions. He would be questioning the whereabouts of his two younger sons.

"Pa will be angry, Elijah," Jeremiah began. "It was wrong to go to Salmon River. That man would've hurt us and taken our horses. I was scared."

"I know, Jeremiah." The scene was vivid in his mind. Elijah was sickened by his own helplessness. He could still smell—was he imagining it?—the foul stench of Amos Finn's breath; he could feel the twisting grip of Finn's grimy hand on his shirt. All the way home he had been rethinking it, imagining how he should have dealt with Finn, how he could have fought back. A quick twist, a punch to Finn's protruding middle, a well-placed kick surely could have brought the man down. But that opportunity was lost, and Elijah's burning ears were proof he'd not look for another opportunity. He was disgusted with himself, ashamed he had hung limp as a rag while Amos Finn half choked him.

The truth was clear: Elijah didn't have the slightest idea how to defend himself, and he knew it. He shook his head at the thought that he could ever go into battle armed with a rifle, intent on killing other men. What might have occurred if Jamie hadn't intervened? He could imagine the embarrassment—and the pain. He couldn't wield a scythe, he couldn't plow a straight row, and he couldn't protect himself, his brother, or their horses against assault.

"Thee must not feel ashamed, Elijah," Jeremiah said. "Thee did as we have been taught. Violence is a sin against God, Pa says. Jamie's actions were an abomination in the sight of God. God will punish him!" Jeremiah looked at his brother with eyes wide, eyebrows arched.

"Stop it!" snapped Elijah. "If not for Jamie, Amos Finn would have beaten me half to death, and thee as well. Jamie saved us—he faced danger on our behalf. There is no greater friendship than that."

"But Pa says..." Jeremiah began.

"Pa is wrong about this, and he is wrong about Jamie," Elijah said. "I cannot accept that God will punish someone who protects another, even if it requires force, and neither should thee." Jeremiah turned away, and Elijah snapped the reins, urging Esther and Ruth to pick up speed. Peru Village was just ahead, and the sooner they got home, the better.

As the wagon approached Elmore's brick store, one kind of tension gave way to another—the familiar edifices of Peru Village spoke of safety to Elijah, but he dreaded explaining the day's events to his father. There would be no getting around it. The decisions to sell the wheat, to befriend the Aikin's boys, to go to Salmon River Settlement—had been his and his alone. He had forgotten all about returning with sugar and molasses. He had not arrived home in time for meeting. He was no doubt a failure in God's eyes as he would be in his father's. He was not sure which was worse.

Asa Elmore stood just outside the double front doors, hands on his hips, as if he had been waiting for them. Elijah pulled up to the water pump in front of the store. Jeremiah jumped down and pumped water into wooden buckets for Esther and Ruth, who drank willingly.

"Your pa was here awhile back," said Asa Elmore. "He was looking for the two of you. Seems David Cochran paid him a visit and gave him some upsetting news. He didn't say what it was, but he said he needed to find you and your brother."

"Did he hear our whereabouts from David Cochran?" Elijah asked.

"He said he feared you two had come under the influence of some bad boys and had run off. He was afraid for your safety and said if I saw you I should send you home straight away. So, that's the message I have for you. It's a shame your pa and I didn't have more time to talk, though," Elmore added. "I had some things to discuss with him. But what I have to say he'll learn soon enough, I suppose."

"Come, Jeremiah. We'd best go home and face Pa."

"Those horses look plumb wrung out," Elmore said, "like they've been running all day. I'd offer you some feed for them, but then you'd be later still."

"Thank thee just the same," Elijah said. "Get on, Jeremiah. Pa wants us home."

Jeremiah slid the buckets, nearly empty, from under the noses of Esther and Ruth and returned them to the platform near the pump. He climbed on the wagon and Elijah pulled away. Asa Elmore waved as they started across the bridge toward the Union Road.

As Esther and Ruth pulled the wagon with renewed vigor up the driveway, Elijah had a sinking feeling. They're anxious to get to the barn, he thought, but that's the last place I want to be. By now, his father and Israel would be there, the milking and feeding would be underway, and Elijah knew the topic of their discussion: the two missing brothers.

Thick smoke rolled out of the chimney at the house; Rebecca was stoking the fire in preparation for cooking dinner. Everything was as it should be in late afternoon. Elijah wished he and Jeremiah might slip silently into their places without anyone noticing, but he knew they couldn't, despite the fact he had been praying for it since they had left Peru Village. That he had been praying at all rather surprised him.

"I'll stable the horses, Elijah," said Jeremiah. His eyes were wide, his skin pale, and Elijah knew his brother hoped to avoid the coming confrontation. "I'll join thee as soon as the horses are wiped down and combed and fed."

"All right," said Elijah. "I'll see thee inside, then." He passed the reins to his brother and climbed down. He strode to the barn and paused with his hands on the rough wooden handle, looked back at Jeremiah, now approaching the stable door, then heaved his body weight and slid the door open on its track.

The barn interior was dark. Only a few flickering lanterns provided light for late afternoon chores. Elijah nearly ran into Israel before he saw him, his great bulk bent over a feeding trough, loading hay for the cows.

"Well, then, the missing ones have come home," Israel said. "I'd think thee would have stayed away a bit longer and avoided chores altogether." He straightened, put his hands on his hips, and viewed his brother in a way that made Elijah take a backward step. For a moment, in memory, Elijah could see Amos Finn in a similar stance, about to throttle him. But as frightening as the experience at Salmon River had been, Elijah somehow felt braver here, even in the presence of an agitated Israel. He tried to meet his brother's stare with one of equal intensity.

"If we are late for chores, Israel Hoag, it is because we have learned our lessons from thee. Many were the days we accomplished our work and thy work because thee was absent from us."

"Pa was worried sick for thy safety when he heard from David Cochran. And allowing the wheat to be sold to soldiers will cause great embarrassment for our family. Thee might have considered more carefully knowing my present situation."

At that moment, the far door slid open and Ben Hoag strode in. All Elijah could see was his dark form moving their way. Jeremiah appeared at the door behind his father, but stayed at the opening. Elijah tugged at the fabric of his shirt, damp with perspiration, which had begun to scratch his neck. He swallowed. His mouth had gone dry.

"Elijah Hoag, thee had better have answers for my questions," called Ben Hoag, coming down the center alley of the barn, "and better answers than thy brother could provide."

He loomed over Elijah. "I've spent the better part of this day searching and inquiring of everyone thy whereabouts." Ben reached out and cupped his open palm under Elijah's chin and lifted it, as if Elijah were a small child. "And what troubles me more than thee feeding an army with our wheat, and running our horses into the ground, and putting thyself and thy brother into mortal danger, is I could only find out about my sons' welfare from world's people!" Elijah tried to draw back against the rising volume of his father's voice, but Ben held his chin fast.

"Pa, I…" Elijah began, but he couldn't move his jaw to speak.

"How, for the love of God, could thee allow Cochran to buy our wheat?" shouted Ben, squeezing Elijah's jaw. "Why did thee not have the presence of mind to speak up for thyself and stand for what thee believes? Does thee not even know what thee believes?"

Elijah stepped back and his father let go of his chin. "Pa, it is our duty as Americans to help fight this threat to our freedom and…"

"Fight?" roared Benjamin Hoag. "Has thee forgotten thyself and who thee has been raised to be? Thy actions have supported a cause of death and destruction, nothing more. Now I must go to the monthly meeting in humiliation to beg forgiveness on thy behalf and promise this will never occur again. And the leaders will look at me, a new overseer, and shake their heads at my inability to control my wayward son. My tenure as overseer is in jeopardy thanks to thee and thy fight for freedom. What has thee to say?"

"Pa, I wished to do our part to protect the freedom which is God's gift. Why, John Keese himself said that…"

"What has John Keese to do with our family? John Keese is yet one more worldly influence on thee and thy sensibility. To suggest God would assent to violence is blasphemous, a defilement of the Christ of peace within us! I'll hear no more of John Keese!"

"But Pa," Elijah continued, unable to stop himself, "I think John Keese wishes to speak with thee about my obtaining an apprenticeship with him. He told Israel days ago, and I think he means for me to help him at Goshen. I cannot be sure as yet, but I…"

"Elijah," Ben said, poking a big finger into Elijah's

chest, "if thee would spend half as much energy tending to thy proper duties on this farm as thee does wishing and dreaming, thee would be far better off. I thank God every day for one responsible son among my children." Turning toward Israel, Ben said, "Thank God for thee, on whom I can depend to carry the work. Israel, on your shoulders rests the future of this farm!"

Elijah looked at Israel. His brother was bathed in sweat, and his typically robust face was washed of color. He dropped the feed buckets he held and wiped his forehead with the back of his hand; his arms, limp at his sides, hung motionless as his fists clenched and unclenched. "Pa," Israel began, "I have something I need tell thee. I have come to love a girl and wish to marry her."

Ben's face brightened. "Joyous news, son! God be praised! Thee have kept it well hidden from us! Whose daughter from among the Friends is she? Will thee plan to come before the next Monthly Meeting with your request?" His smile broadened as he waited for Israel's response.

"She is not from among the Friends, Pa. She is Martha Elmore, daughter of Asa Elmore, the storekeeper in Peru Village."

As the meaning of Israel's words hit their mark, Ben's countenance slowly fell, his smile faded into furrowed brows, and his lips curled into a grimace. He reached for the wooden stanchion for support. "Israel—son—thee cannot be serious…"

"I am, Pa. I have never been surer of anything in my

life."

"To carry out such a marriage would result in thy disownment, not to mention the shame thee would bring on the family. Why, the meeting will not stand for it! I'll not stand for it!"

"It is not for the meeting or for thee to decide, Pa," Israel said. "I will follow my heart. Martha is the woman I love and the one I shall marry. I shall not be swayed by the meeting."

"Well, if thee be swayed or not, they will visit," snapped Ben. "Other overseers like myself will come and talk sense to thee, and…"

"My mind is made up, Pa. I'll not receive visitors from the meeting, and I'll discuss it no further with thee. Asa Elmore has offered me a room above the store for now, and I shall move there at first opportunity. Martha's and my betrothal will take place after harvest, in the new Methodist-Episcopal Church where she belongs. She is a Christian girl, Pa, and that to me is what matters."

"She is from world's people, outside our faith!" shouted Ben.

"She is the woman with whom I'll spend the rest of my life," replied Israel, his voice low, and measured, and calm. Elijah noted the color had returned to his brother's face. His hands were now on his hips, and he looked his father firmly in the eye as he spoke.

"But what of our farm…our life?" Ben asked, his voice softening, cracking.

"Thee has Elijah and Jeremiah to carry on the farm,"

said Israel.

Elijah was conscious that he, too, was perspiring, though these last words from Israel made him shudder as if a cold wind had blown through the barn. There it was. The harsh reality of his brother's departure was that it would drop the future of the farm on his reluctant shoulders. Israel would attain what he wanted in all of this, but Elijah was about to inherit unacceptable responsibility and position. He felt something brush his sleeve as Jeremiah arrived to stand beside him. Elijah glanced at his father and was startled by the strange expression on his face—Benjamin Hoag was smiling.

Ben's gaze fell on each of his sons in turn. Elijah was confused by the quiet calm which had befallen his father. Ben closed his eyes and elevated his head. "I was certain Elijah provided me my only cross to bear, but now I see I am blessed again by my son, Israel, in whom I had placed my faith and my hope," he said. Elijah braced himself for another explosion, but it failed to come. "I am enriched by this heavy cross I bear, as was Christ himself, staggering under it to the hill of Golgotha. I am, in my suffering, ever nearer to the Savior." He opened his eyes, and tears rolled down his cheeks. He wiped them with a massive hand. "I am baptized again by this, my sons—washed clean by the refining power of the holy spirit of God. A lowly man like I am doesn't deserve such a blessing." He walked to the side door of the barn, turning as he reached it. "Though two of my sons desert me, I am ever closer to the Inner Light, shining within me. I am at peace. And I have yet one son I can still depend upon." He stepped outside.

"Pa…wait!" Jeremiah said, pushing past his brothers and running out the open doorway.

Israel stood a long moment and stared toward the door. He drew in a deep breath and let it out, bending to pick up the feed buckets he had dropped. "Come Elijah, there are chores to finish. Rebecca will be waiting supper."

"What now, Israel?" Elijah asked.

"Chores, Elijah. The work of this day must be completed. That is all I know to do this moment." He began to fill the nearest trough with feed.

Elijah took a long handled scraper and began cleaning out the alley and stalls. With each pull of the handle he recalled the awful events of the day—the giving of the wheat to David Cochran, the unplanned trip to Salmon River, the embarrassing altercation with Amos Finn, and, now, Israel's confession to their father. The quiet predictability of his life was shaken. All he wanted to do was complete the work, go to the house, and collapse into bed. He was exhausted. His head and eyes ached. Rebecca would have something to say about his missing a meal she had held back for him, no doubt, but Elijah only wanted to blot out the day and retreat into the safety of sleep. He was thankful to be able to control something in an otherwise disturbing day.

Elijah completed the barn chores, trudged to the house, and crept up the back stairway. He threw off his clothes, donned a nightshirt, and fell into his bed, falling almost immediately into an exhausted sleep.

CHAPTER 11

Elijah sat bolt upright in bed, gasping for breath, feeling frightened and disoriented. He shook his head and tried to strain his eyes against the darkness. Had he only just fallen asleep? He wiped his eyes and found them to be wet, his forehead soaked with perspiration. The images he had seen terrified him. They were still in his head. Walking through a desolate landscape, blackened tree stumps covering the ground, gray mist in the air, he had been trying to locate his family. He had called in his dream for each of them—*Pa! Israel! Rebecca! Jeremiah!*—but they were nowhere to be found in the hazy atmosphere, laden with the smell of musket smoke and another smell he could not identify, but which unnerved him. The ground was covered with rubble, with the stones of foundations cast asunder. The last name he called was his mother's, and it was what had awakened him, the sound of his own voice calling out *Ma!*

But more than remembering the images, Elijah was filled with an overwhelming sense of death, an overpowering feeling that something was wrong, that someone he knew had died. He looked out the east window of his bedroom. The slightest trace of pink outlined the mountains of Vermont as morning approached. His mind raced, trying to make sense of the images, so like the ones he had discussed days ago with Aunt Winifred. Aunt Winifred! Dear God, could it be Aunt Winifred had died, or was near death? Elijah swung his legs out of the bed and started to pull on his clothes, but then he stopped. How foolish to think he could grope his way into the stable, outfit a horse, and ride away without someone noticing. He leaned back on the bed, then lurched forward again. Ma! The last name he had spoken had been her name. He pulled on his trousers and crept out of his room.

Elijah eased himself down the stairs, trying to avoid the squeaking, creaking boards, loosened over the years by the great weight of his brother and father as they climbed to the second floor. He paused at the bottom, listening for signs he may have awakened anyone. Rebecca, who slept in the downstairs bedroom off the dining room, was snoring softly, nearly in time with the ticking of the dining room clock.

Elijah padded through the kitchen, past the fireplace, red coals still visible in the dark firebox. He stood at the doorway of the small room off the kitchen, held his breath, and listened for any sound from within. At first he heard nothing, and this filled him with dread. His dream had come true, and now he would be the one to discover its reality. A cold sweat coated his forehead as he imagined his mother's lifeless body.

Then, he heard a small sound, a drawn breath, followed by the whispery breathing of his mother. Elijah exhaled in relief, and quietly turned to go back to his room and wait for daylight so he could get to his Aunt Winifred.

"Elijah?" called a soft voice. "Is it thee, son?"

Elijah stepped inside the room. "Yes, Ma, I've come to check on thee, 'tis all."

"I awoke when thee called out my name," said his mother. "Were I a little stronger, I'd have come to thee. I was reminded of when thee were a small boy and would call my name in the night."

Elijah stepped to the foot of his mother's bed, and then felt his way around the side to the chair. He sat and stared into the dark place on the bed where he knew his mother lay. The sky was lighter, but it was still dark in the room, and his mother was only a shadow. He leaned closer to better hear her. "How are thee, Mother?"

"In truth, I feel improved, even at this early hour of the day. What made thee cry out?"

"A dream awakened me, is all," Elijah replied.

"What sort of dream would make thee cry out with such fear in thy voice?"

Elijah squinted at the dark shape on the bed so as to see his mother, but the light was still too dim. "It was a confusing dream where I tried to find all my family in a world of death and destruction, but try as I might, I could not find them. It was cold and frightening. I was alone."

"Well, thee has found me now, son. How long have thee had these dreams?"

"Months…perhaps a year. They make me feel empty inside, like I have lost something or someone valuable. They frighten me and make me think of death."

"Whose death?"

"I do not know," Elijah said. "Tonight I feared it was thy death, or perhaps Aunt Winifred's."

"Well, we know whose it is not, then, don't we?" Elijah heard a smile in her voice. "Does thee think these dreams will come to pass?"

"I fear that they will, just as my cousin's dreams have," he answered.

"Ah, yes. Cousin Joseph. All his visions have not been frightening prophecies, thee knows."

"My dreams seem so," Elijah said. "I fear them and what they mean."

"As did Cousin Joseph fear his," said his mother. "But as the circumstances of his life changed, so did the visions. Has thee told thy father of these prophecies?"

"My father would think I was inventing them. My father doubts I am worthy of such visions."

"Thy father, despite being a good man, is often quick to judge. He is deep in the faith, and expects others, especially his family, to be as he is."

"My father is convinced I am far from the Light, that I have friends who are far from the Light, that I shall never find the Light." Elijah felt desperation creeping in.

"There are differences among Friends thy father does not acknowledge. I know of this first hand. There are points of faith upon which he and I disagree."

"I cannot seem to find the easy way to the Light he

does, or Israel, or Jeremiah, for that matter."

"Thee must stop trying to be like them, Elijah. It is not in adopting another Friend's way that we embrace the Light. Believe instead that in seeking, we are found. It is not that we find the Light, but that we put ourselves in such a place as to be found. I daresay the Light is manifested in thee in the midst of thy denial."

"Aunt Winifred says I need only open my eyes."

"The eyes of thy heart, yes, and thy ears for the hearing. Go into the silence and listen, and God the Light will speak. It is as Elias Hicks has said."

"That is a name which infuriates my father," said Elijah.

"Your father disagrees with his preaching. Brother Elias believes in simpler ways, in a simpler relationship without the layers of rules and regulations. Simple devotion to the Light, much like our Society was in the beginning."

"Aunt Winifred speaks well of him."

"Yes. Many of us feel what he preaches is worthy of consideration." She paused. "Besides, he is a kinsman of mine."

"He is what?" said Elijah.

"Elias Hicks is the half-brother to my mother; he is my uncle and your great-uncle."

Elijah was dumbfounded. "Why have I never heard this?"

"Your father has forbidden me to speak of it. Part of the agreement in our marriage is that I'll not dwell on my beliefs concerning Elias Hicks. So I keep them to myself, in silence."

"So what he preaches is not evil?"

"We are led to interpret the Light each for ourselves. It is not for us to judge or question the revelation of others, unless it flies in the face of all bible truths. Uncle Elias's teachings reach back to a simpler time when our focus was more personal, concerned with each person's relationship to his Inner Christ and in how that relationship spoke to our community. But time changes beliefs, and beliefs must adjust. Thy father has embraced changes fraught with rules to clarify and instruct. It is in this that he parts company with Uncle Elias."

"Then my friends are not evil?" said Elijah.

"If thee mean the Greens and others like them, no, I do not believe so. And neither would Uncle Elias."

Elijah felt as though he was at the beginning of understanding something new, but his face burned as his mother said, "Thy father came to me last evening and told me of thy brother's intent, and of thy talk of John Keese's proposition, or hint of one."

"Yes, Ma, but my father has made me feel this is a foolish idea, only a dream, and I..."

"And what have I told thee of thy dreams?" interrupted his mother. "When your life takes new directions, there will be new dreams—dreams you'd never anticipated. Go in to God, Elijah. Seek His direction in prayer and He will guide you. Be open to God. Be open to your dreams, the good and the bad."

Elijah rubbed his eyes and yawned. It was beginning to be lighter in the room, and he could make out his mother's face.

"There is still time to rest a bit before morning chores, Elijah. Thee and I are alike, as alike as your father is to Israel and Jeremiah. Thy father feels my illnesses have been punishment for my opposition to his beliefs. He might be surprised to hear I am feeling much better today than I have in weeks." There was enough light now that Elijah could see a faint smile. "Stop punishing thyself, my son. Go out and seek God's way. Listen and you will know." She coughed. "I'm tired now." She closed her eyes, and her gentle breathing resumed. Elijah leaned down, brushing his mother's forehead with his lips.

The sun was not up, but there was enough light for Elijah to easily find his way back upstairs. He would lie down awhile and listen for Jeremiah and Israel and their father to descend the stairs. He made up his mind not to sleep, but closed his eyes as he listened.

CHAPTER 12

Sixth Day September 9, 1814

Elijah opened his eyes to blinding sunlight streaming in the east window of his bedroom. For a moment he lay still, trying to get his bearings. Something seemed different, but he couldn't quite identify what it was. Then he realized. It was the smell of food cooking—breakfast—an aroma he had not smelled from this location of the house for many years. He inhaled, enjoying the rich smell of bacon frying. Suddenly the reality struck him: the sun was up, breakfast was cooking, and he had overslept morning chores!

For the second time in only a few hours, Elijah bolted from his bed, surprised to discover he was wearing his trousers pulled up over his nightshirt. He yanked his stockings on, then his boots, and dashed down the stairs.

He burst into the kitchen to find Rebecca stirring pans over the cook fire. She looked him up and down, her hand on her cheek, struggling not to laugh. "Well, slug-a-bed," she said, "was the sun finally high enough in the sky to coax thee down from thy chamber? Is the nightshirt in case thee need a brief nap later in the morning, in the haymow, perhaps?" Rebecca threw her head back and laughed heartily. “Father, Israel, and Jeremiah were going to wait chores for thee but decided it might interfere with lunch, so they went ahead without thee!” She seemed particularly jolly this day.

“Now don’t be too hard on my boy,” came a voice from the adjoining room. Elijah heard movement, and his mother appeared at the door, in a nightdress, wrapped in a shawl. “He checked on me early this morning and needed his rest,” his mother said, smiling at Elijah. She steadied herself in the doorway. “I’m a bit weak still,” she said, “but I believe I shall rejoin the living in a few days.”

As Rebecca went to help their mother, Elijah opened the door and raced down the steps. “I’ll be back soon,” he said over his shoulder. He was intent on getting a horse and riding as fast as he could to Aunt Winifred.

He sprinted to the stable and found Esther inside, munching oats, with Ruth nowhere to be seen. Puzzled, he turned in time to see their small wagon approaching on Rogers Road, with Ruth pulling and Jeremiah at the reins. Elijah ran to the end of the drive to wait. Why would Jeremiah be out at this hour?

Jeremiah guided Ruth into the drive and stopped next to Elijah. “Mornin’, Elijah,” he said. “We missed thee at chores.”

“Where has thee been?” Elijah asked, grasping Ruth’s harness, patting her side, ignoring his brother’s comment.

“I’ve been to Aunt Winifred’s, bringing grain for her horses. Pa was so upset last night he forgot to tell us she was nearly out. He sent me this morning after I fed the stock. Is thee sick?"

"Not sick. Worried about Aunt Winifred."

"I just left her. She is well—a little bent over with her rheumatism, but, as she says, it's early in the day, and she improves with each passing hour. Why is thee concerned for her?"

"I awoke thinking of her," Elijah answered as his attention was drawn south down the Rogers Road by a cloud of dust, the sound of horses and wagons, and the sight of many men on foot. "What could this be?" he wondered aloud. He and Jeremiah watched as the crowd approached, twenty or thirty men carrying guns, walking in threes and fours in no particular formation. Elijah's heart jumped, as he thought they might be British, but since they were not wearing uniforms and certainly did not look to be a polished army, he realized they weren't. Plus, they were coming from the south. He looked back toward the barns and saw his father, standing in the yard, two grain buckets in his hands, watching.

"Hello, young fellows!" called a man toward the front of the procession. He shifted his gun to his left hand and waved with his right. The group slowed to a stop, and the man extended his hand. "Name's Alton Macguire," he said, smiling in a friendly way. "We're the advance company for General Strong of the Vermont militia. He's a day behind us leading a contingent of men bound for Plattsburgh. We're seeking the Guilliland homestead on the Lake Road, but I fear we've strayed out of our way. Our destination is the Salmon River Settlement."

"Thee is out of the way, it's true," said Elijah. "This is the Peru Union. Thee have come far up from the lake."

"I thought as much," said Macguire. He gestured to a rotund man near the front of the assembly, drinking from a canteen and chewing on what appeared to be some sort of smoked meat. "My second-in-command here urged us to seek higher ground to gain an overlook. We've no maps, but only the directions offered by Vermonters who have already been involved in the siege of Plattsburgh. We failed to allow for the confusion of roads hereabouts. Let's hope the British have as much difficulty finding their way as we have." He smiled, but his eyes were bloodshot, his face drawn. "Soldiering is not our calling, you see, but a necessity brought on by the times."

"Thee will need to retrace thy steps," said Elijah. "If thee continues this way, thee will miss the Guilliland place entirely, even though thee might finally arrive at Salmon River. Once in view of the lake, seek the road running north along the shore; it will lead thee to the Guilliland homestead."

"Well, we need to find Guilliland's," said Macguire. "He has a store of arms for incoming militia. Some of our fellows have only their fowling pieces. We fear we'll need proper muskets for the job that awaits us."

Elijah remembered his travels of the previous day, the threat of danger, the nearness to the fighting. Jamie came briefly to his mind. He wondered if he should tell these men about his friend and ask that they seek him out. Elijah was confused at his feelings. Part of him was relieved he was safe at home, not marching off into danger. Yet still he felt guilty, knowing Jamie was out there. His mind drifted further, and he saw flashes of gunfire and thick white smoke. Though the vision lasted only seconds, Elijah felt cold, overcome by sadness and dread. He wondered if this group of men, obviously townspeople and farmers like the Hoags, were marching to their deaths. It occurred to Elijah they might be the reason for his death-tainted dreams of last night.

"Elijah," said Jeremiah, "yonder comes Pa."

Ben Hoag strode up the driveway, his mouth a tight line, his brow furrowed. He came to stand between Elijah and Jeremiah, facing Alton Macguire, who immediately smiled and extended his hand. Ben Hoag did not return the gesture.

"What brings thee to our gate?" Ben asked.

Macguire's smile faded, and he withdrew his hand. "We're Vermonters, aiming to do our part to fend off the British invasion of Plattsburgh and our valley," he said. "Our apology to you for intruding on your community, but we have lost our way."

"Thee has lost thy way in more than this," Ben remarked. "My sons and I, my family, my community, do not support war and its violence by any means. I will thank thee to leave us to our work."

"We know of the ways of the Quakers," said Macguire, "and we respect them. We are from the Charlotte region, not far distant from Ferrisburg, where there is a community like yourselves."

"Many of our numbers hail from Ferrisburg," said Ben, "not that it is of any concern to thee. Thee knows, then, we reject killing outright and find it an abomination, a sin on the spirit. We shall have no contact with those involved. God be merciful to thee. Come, boys."

Ben turned toward the house and started down the drive, and Jeremiah followed. Elijah wanted to say more to the man, to apologize for his father's abruptness. He opened his mouth to speak, but Ben turned and addressed him. "Elijah, come. Breakfast waits, then we must be about our work before the rains come again. We've no more time to waste with world's people and their ways."

"We thank you for your help, lad," said Alton Macguire. "Sorry for the trouble." He turned to the party behind him. "Turn about, fellows. Back the way we've come."

Elijah watched as the men turned the supply wagon around. Others mounted horses. The men on foot, heads shaking, reversed directions. Elijah heard them mumbling, but couldn't make out what they said, though one man's voice stood out: "An idiot could see we were too far from the lake, for God's sake." Alton Macguire watched his company assemble, then gave the order to proceed. He nodded at Elijah and walked to the side of the group, but faster, gradually taking his place at the front.

"Elijah," drifted Jeremiah's voice from the house, "Pa says come now!"

Elijah, standing in the road, looked back at his house, at the newly harvested fields surrounding it. Smoke rose up from the chimney. The large, squarish house seemed part of the earth, the rough-sided barns were familiar and comforting.

Sudden shouts from the Vermont militia men drew Elijah's attention. The dust cloud was rising around their feet again, and Elijah could hear laughter. The last irregular line of men looked back in his direction and threw up their hands in a final wave. It reminded Elijah of Jamie's wave, just before he disappeared down the riverbank with the Aikin's boys. He felt a sudden, overpowering urge to rush after them, to fall in step and take his place among them, these men who were just common men, like the Hoags, the Greens, the Keeses, the Elmores. He took a step toward them, but hesitated, his courage ebbing away as he remembered their destination.

"Elijah!" boomed the great voice from the kitchen door. One final look up the road, and Elijah started down the drive to breakfast. He would need nourishment to prepare for yet another day of work.

CHAPTER 13

Seventh Day, September 10, 1814

With slow methodical strokes, Elijah scraped the barn floor. He focused on every shred of straw bedding, every dropped kernel of grain, every pile of dung, as he whisked it all into the central alley of the big barn. He had done this job since he was old enough to struggle with the weight of the wide, metal blade, its gray, wooden handle worn so smooth with age it slipped time and time again from his grasp. He could do it without thinking—a good thing, since he could not get the events of the previous morning out of his mind. The sight of the Vermont militia, their waves and smiles, his father's unfriendly demeanor, his own conflicted emotions of guilt and fear confused him.

Elijah had an unsettled feeling. Perhaps it was the weather. The slate-gray sky promised rain again, and soon. One job after another had been interrupted or prevented thanks to the frequent deluges of the past days. Perhaps it was his state of fatigue—their father had worked them long and hard the previous day, completing the harvest. Elijah believed his muscles would never stop aching. And again he had awakened in the night in the midst of dreams he could not remember, dreams that left him overcome with a cold emptiness. Elijah tried to tell himself it was all just the leftover feelings about his trip to Salmon River Settlement, caused by the reality of imminent invasion by an overwhelming force—and the fear that his own safety, and the safety of his home, his family, were in jeopardy.

But what could the British possibly want with Peru Village or the Quaker Union? Surely they wouldn't stray so far from the lake? They would plunge in unspeakable numbers along the shore and overwhelm the tiny force of defenders—too many men who were like those he had seen yesterday on the Rogers Road, men who looked more comfortable behind the counter of a general store than behind a gun. The British would storm the forts, burn Plattsburgh, and continue south, unimpeded. Then they would be gone, and life could return to normal—at least for a time.

"Elijah?" called a voice from the sliding door at the end of the barn…a voice Elijah knew, yet did not know. Not his father or his brothers, but familiar somehow. He looked down the shadowy alley toward the doorway. Three figures stood there. Elijah stopped raking. For some reason his heart was pounding.

"Yes?" he answered. "Who be ye?"

The tallest shadow stepped forward. "Hank Averill, Elijah. Hank and Jonathan and Hiram, from Aikin's Company." The boys walked down the center of the barn. Hank shoved his hat back on his forehead and pushed his glasses up on his nose. The others stood at his side, their eyes downcast. Elijah noticed a change in their appearance. Their clothing was filthy, ripped in places, reeking of gunpowder. Their faces were smudged and scratched. Jonathan wasn't wearing shoes.

Elijah's heart leaped ahead. "Is Jamie with thee?" Elijah felt great relief that his friend would be home now, probably giving a grand description of his adventures to his family. He leaned on his scraper, already planning to find Jamie later and hear for himself the great tale of adventure. No one could tell a story like Jamie!

"It's why we've come to the Union, to bring news of Jamie to his family and to you," Hank began, speaking slowly as though searching for every word. "Elijah, we were given permission to come to Peru Union by Captain Aikin to tell you…to tell you…" His voice drifted off. He cleared his throat and pushed his glasses further up on his nose. "Elijah, Jamie was killed two days ago, along with our companion, young Peters. They were struck by cannon fire—grape shot—while defending the bridge in Plattsburgh. Jamie stepped in front of Peters to shield him, but it was too much for them to survive. I'm sorry, Elijah."

Elijah stared at Hank. Jamie dead? Killed on the same day they had arrived at Salmon River Settlement? He felt the rake leave his hands, heard it hit the ground. Surely he had misunderstood. There was buzzing in his ears, tightness around his neck as if he were being choked. He shook his head to clear it, but couldn't. His stomach lurched, as though he had been kicked. His arms began shaking violently, and he crossed them over his chest to quiet them, his hands gripping his own shoulders. "No," Elijah said, "that can't be! Not Jamie..."

"He was a brave fellow," said Hiram. "We liked him. And our friend Peters was younger than us, just a boy."

"We didn't figure on this kind of thing happening," said Jonathan. "We thought we was too quick, too smart. But Jamie and Peters, they got out from behind the barricades we'd thrown up. It just happened so quick and all."

"Well, this is what I had known would happen," intruded a deep voice. Elijah jumped when he heard it. Ben Hoag had come in from the side door. "Pity to the man who deals in war and killing, for he will receive God's justice."

Elijah turned to face his father, unable to believe what he had just heard.

"How can thee say that?" Elijah said. "God's justice? What does God have to do with this? Jamie was my friend."

"That lad has been doomed from the beginning," continued Ben, shaking his head. "His family did not guide and instruct him in the true way of the Friends, so God's will is done."

"But Pa," Elijah said, his voice rising. "Time and time again he defended me, and he died defending another. Isn't it said of our Lord that the greatest love one can have is to lay down his life for his friends, as He did?"

"Elijah," Ben said, his voice calm and hollow. "Thee should not speak the name of our Lord in association with those whose sin has brought on their demise."

"What sin has Jamie committed but to give his life to save another?" Elijah sobbed, tears running down his face. "I cannot stand thy narrow belief!"

"Thee says these things," continued Ben, as though he was not hearing, "because of thy association with Jamie Green and with the Green family. Their worldly ways shame our Society and have cost them their son. Had they brought him up as thee have been brought up…"

"I cannot listen to thee!" screamed Elijah. "We must help them!"

"We will not help them," Ben said. "The Greens must now feel the sting of God's judgment. This time of suffering will be a baptism for them. They will be deepened because of it, thank God. Why, I shall visit them in my capacity as overseer and endeavor to point this out to them. Perhaps they will turn toward the Light they've shunned."

"I am sick at thy words," Elijah said, his voice shaking, his throat tight. "I am disgusted and ashamed. I am going to Jamie's family."

"I'll not allow it!" Ben stated, his girth filling the small doorway. "God will punish thee as well!"

"Then let thy God punish me," shouted Elijah. "'Tis not thy God I serve." He kicked the rake aside, sprinted the length of the barn, and exited the far door. Great sobs choked him, tears blinded him as he raced out the drive, running faster than he ever had before—running from his father, running from his father's God. Up the Rogers Road he sped, lungs burning, heart pounding. But instead of taking the road to the Green place, he turned without thinking onto the back road to Goshen.

Elijah gripped the earthenware mug with both hands and let the cool water flow down his throat. He paused between swallows to gasp. Hot sweat rolled in rivers down his face, in his ears, stinging his eyes. Aunt Winifred sat beside him in her rickety wooden chair under a large pine. He had poured out the story of Jamie's death while she had listened, her hand pressed against her chest. Then he had collapsed, sides heaving, at her feet. Without speaking, she rose and walked to her well, drew him the cup of water, and returned to offer it to him.

Elijah drained the cup and set it on the grass, noticing as he did so the gentle movement of the chair's rockers. He leaned back, resting on his elbows. The grass felt cool, the earth soft. He could no longer hear his heart pounding nor feel the throbbing in his neck. Aunt Winifred's hands were folded in her lap as she gazed out at the fields and pastures. The sky was slate gray; the thick, lowering clouds cloaked the sun.

"This time of day is my favorite," Aunt Winifred said. "Even on such a dismal day, the light shines through. There is great promise, I think."

"Jamie is dead, Aunt. How can it be a day of promise?" Elijah asked.

"Each day brings with it the chance, the hope, of

something good," Aunt Winifred replied. She closed her eyes and rocked gently. "Even in the midst of sorrow."

"Jamie is dead, and I could have prevented it," said Elijah, his voice breaking.

"Thee must not blame thyself in thy grief," said Aunt Winifred. "Young Jamie Green chose his own way. He responded to a call from deep within himself, a feeling only satisfied by action."

"But I could have forced him to return home with us."

"Thee could not. Sad, but thee could not," said his aunt. "He followed an impulse stronger than thee."

"Pa says he brought this upon himself by his failure to live according to the rules of the Friends," said Elijah. "Pa says it is God's punishment."

"Thy father and thy father's rules cannot judge the impulses of Jamie Green, and no one can know the heart of God. There is no sin when thee respond to the urging in thy heart for a cause that is right. "

"Even if it means killing another?" Elijah asked.

Aunt Winifred, eyes closed, rocked in silence. Then she stopped rocking, opened her eyes, and looked at Elijah. "I have seen much in my time. I was born when the Society of Friends was young. In the early years of my life, many men who professed to be among the Friends had associations with the military. In time, the majority have come to hold to our testimony of peace.

"But seeds of change are sown with the passing of time," she continued. "Perhaps there are moments when we must respond to our heart's demand even if we must shun our pacifism. Perhaps Jamie Green had come to a crossing in his life's path, and chose to step away from the peaceful ways of the Friends." She smiled at Elijah. "We love our simple ways, but at times life is not so simple. All we can do is go in prayer to the Light and seek truth for ourselves, then respond to the truth as best we can. Sharing that truth may persuade the community to change. Or it may result in the loss of members from our fold. Thee may not see truth as does another, but thee must stay attached to the Light to discern thy own truth, as the petals are attached on a daisy to its center, each anchored independent of the other."

"So I may find my own way on a path I choose?" asked Elijah.

"Aye, such is my belief. Thee seek a definite way, dear one, yet life confronts us with many ways to choose. There are varieties of gifts that assist us on our way. Thy dreams are such a gift…and thy sensitive heart."

"The dreams are still troubling to me."

"And they shall be, until thee embrace them, good and bad. Seek the Light in the midst of thy dreams, Elijah. Seek and thee will be found, and thee will learn thy own truth." She paused and coughed softly.

Elijah felt a strange release inside, a sudden peace. He wondered if the Light could reveal itself in his aunt's words, awakening the Christ in himself…the One he'd so often denied.

"Aunt, there is something I must do," Elijah said, getting to his feet.

"Yes, dear one, I should say there is."

He kissed his aunt on the forehead and walked back the way he'd come.

Elijah followed the long lane toward the Green farm. After talking to his aunt, he felt sure of his decision, and he needed to find Sarah. Her brother had been his best friend. He could no longer remain silent or uninvolved.

As he neared the house, he heard the clatter of a wagon. Sarah, in the wagon seat, drove from the back of the house, the horses already stepping high, building speed. She saw Elijah and pulled up beside him. The wagon rattled to an abrupt stop and the horses tossed their heads, looking with bulging eyes as if to ask why they had been asked to run so short a distance.

Sarah's face was puffy, her eyes red-rimmed. "Oh, Elijah," she said, "thee is here. I was bound for thy farm. Such horrible news!" She dropped the reins and began to sob. The horses stepped from side to side, snorting. Elijah jumped to the seat beside Sarah, and she fell against him. He held her as she wept. His mind raced to find words to say, but no words came. All he knew to do was match the tightness of her embrace with his.

"Those boys are here, with Pa," she said after a while, wiping her eyes with the back of her hands. "They are trying to make him understand what's happened. I had to find thee. Please, thee must do something."

"Yes, I know," Elijah said. "I shall go with Hank and the others for Jamie's sake." He pushed away the creeping feeling of doubt. He should have stayed with Jamie in the first place. Now Jamie was gone, and this was what had to be done. He was sure of it. At least, he thought he was.

"I am afraid," said Sarah. "I have lost my brother." She put her hand on his arm. "I couldn't move from this place if I lost thee as well."

"What do you mean, move from this place?" Elijah asked.

"Pa has decided to leave the Union. He is tired of the words being used against him and weary of the discipline threatened by the overseers. We are to leave after the harvest for Pennsylvania to winter with our kin, then go on to the Short Creek Meeting in Ohio in the spring. Pa says we'll have more freedom there."

"But surely you can't go…" Elijah began.

"Pa has sold the farm to one of the Keese brothers. It is decided."

When he held her to console her, Elijah had a strange, wonderful feeling he'd never felt, a feeling of hope that he wouldn't be quite so alone. But this news of her imminent departure struck away that hope, and new thoughts entered his mind.

What did it matter now if he went to war? What did it matter if he were killed? All he had in his life were endless mishaps and failures to live up to his father's expectations. The feeling he might actually have a future with someone had sputtered out like a doused candle. For a fleeting second, he thought he'd felt the Light. But no more.

"Elijah!" called a voice, before he could say something to Sarah that might change her mind. It was Hank, walking up from behind the house. "We are staying here today to help Mr. Green, but tonight we must return to our company. Will you come with us?"

"Yes," said Elijah, and for once, he was sure.

"Intelligence has come to our generals that the British attack is imminent on the land and on the lake," Hank said. "The British navy has been sighted near Chazy. It is felt they will attack together. It may only be a matter of hours before the battle!"

"Elijah, thee must tell thy family," said Sarah.

"No," said Elijah. "My father does not care where I am. I'll lend a hand here, and then go with these fellows tonight."

"First rate!" said Hank. "Jonathan has the musket Jamie used. It shall be yours. Now, let's give a hand to Mr. Green."

Sarah turned the wagon around and drove back toward the barn. Elijah fell in step beside Hank. He felt strong in his decision to act, much as Jamie had days ago, without the consent of his family. He wondered what his father would say about this…his middle son first selling corn to the military, and now taking part in the fight. He would see it as a blessing, no doubt, and feel even closer to God. But in this moment, Elijah felt God was absent, and he was on his own, alone.

"Hank," Elijah began, "if possible, I should like to have a look at that musket."

CHAPTER 14

First Day, September 11, 1814

The air was misty with rain as the boys made their way down the Arthur Road toward the lake. It was first light, and Elijah could clearly see the pale dirt road outlined by the tall, dark pines running along its edge. They walked in silence, he and Hank and Hiram. Jonathan, after helping at Green's farm all the previous day, had said he couldn't go on any longer, but needed to go home. The others had tried to convince him to stay, but to no avail. Elijah's own newly found confidence had begun to waver—if this stalwart young man felt uneasy enough about the impending battle to go home, perhaps he should, too. But then he remembered the parting with his father and thought better of it. He needed to live out the choice he had made, no matter its outcome. What was left for him in any event?

Mr. Green had confirmed what Sarah had said—they would be leaving at the first opportunity to journey to Pennsylvania and then on to Ohio. Sarah had spent most of the afternoon with her father in the house. She had prepared a cold supper for the Aikin's boys and Elijah—cheese and bread—but then had returned inside. There had been no chance to talk, no opportunity to speak to her about what he had been feeling. No chance to say good-bye.

Tossing and turning in the haymow, it seemed he hadn't slept at all when Hank nudged him and said they had to be on their way. They had to rejoin their unit at Salmon River Settlement before midmorning.

The boys half walked, half trotted, along the partially lit road, Hank in the lead, followed by Hiram, and then Elijah. Amazed he was keeping up the pace despite his lack of sleep, Elijah gripped the musket, the one that had been Jamie's. He wondered if that was what strengthened him, knowing the gun had last been in his dead friend's hands.

The road led steadily downhill and would eventually intersect with the Lake Road, not far from Peru Landing, where the Vermont militia had come ashore. Elijah concluded they must be coming near that place as the trees began to widen out from the road and the whole vista of Lake Champlain became visible. A sliver of sky above the Green Mountains of Vermont was illumined by the rising sun, though the sun couldn't penetrate the clouds.

As they reached the Lake Road and looked north, they saw a line of men on the march. Elijah broke into a cold sweat seeing them, but realized they must be Vermont or other local militia bound for Plattsburgh. Still moving at a trot, the boys caught up with the back of the group. Elijah could see they had a common look about them, much like the group of men that had passed their farm two days prior.

"Beg pardon, sir," said Hank to a man at the end of the formation. "From whence do you hail?"

"Essex militia, south down the lake," said the man. "Ahead of us be Vermonters newly arrived at the Landing before sunrise. We're bound for Guilliland's, and then Salmon River. Word has it we'll see a fight today."

"We are three of Aikin's Volunteer Rifle Company," said Hank. "I am Hank, and these are Hiram and Elijah." Elijah only nodded at the man. It was strange to be named one of Aikin's Volunteers.

The man ran a rough hand over his grizzled face, looking the boys over, pausing to scrutinize Elijah's collarless shirt and wide-brimmed hat. He shook his head. "Fall in with us, fellers, and keep up. No time for sociability. We've a distance to go and it's brighter now. If there's to be a battle, sure enough it will start early." He broke into a trot to catch up with a small group of men ahead. Elijah, Hank, and Hiram ran to keep up.

Suddenly the entire column stopped. It was unclear why until a rumbling sound echoed down the lake, out over the water. Elijah's first thought was that it was thunder, until Hiram said, "That be the sound of cannons being scaled."

"What does that mean?" Elijah asked, wondering how far the cannons were, and if they were aimed this way.

"A ship needs to clean out its cannons by exploding charges of gunpowder inside them," said Hank. "That sounded north on the lake, probably the approach of the British navy."

"We could hear it from this distance?" asked Elijah.

"Indeed," said Hank. "Sound travels over the water, and besides, as the crow flies, it is not far from us."

The column had begun to move forward again, faster than before and with a feeling of urgency. Elijah wondered how much longer they had to travel, and he marveled at his own endurance. He had never walked, or run, such a distance in so short a time. He did not feel in the least tired, but instead as if he was being pushed on by an unknown force. He gripped the rifle with both hands, focused his eyes on the men in the column ahead, and ran to keep up.

Elijah lost track of how much time had passed. The sky was fully light, yet shrouded by clouds, and a mist was in the air. A persistent, distant rumble echoed from the north end of the lake, blocked from sight by Valcour Island. Elijah wondered if the misty sky was cannon smoke from the ships the Vermonters said must be engaged off Plattsburgh, or if he saw only low-hanging clouds. All he knew for certain was the longer they pressed north along the lake, the louder and fiercer the rumbling sounded. He thought he could see a homestead ahead, and some barns—no doubt the Guilliland farm.

Suddenly, the not-so-distant explosion of musket fire erupted off to the left, up the Junction Road toward Salmon River Settlement. With a whoop, the head of the group of militia and Vermont volunteers rushed ahead. Hank, Hiram, and Elijah were caught up in the forward rush of men and guns, somewhere in the middle of the throng now. The shouts of the vanguard of the assembly were accompanied by the echoing booms of cannon fire, two shots exploding in close succession. The cannon fire was a distance away, but Elijah realized the cannon would be firing at someone. The place and time of conflict drew near.

"Load your musket!" Hank shouted as he slowed his pace, and others, too, slowed to ready their weapons. Elijah fumbled with the ammo pouch Jamie had carried, pulling out a charge. He unfastened the tie, his fingers shaking uncontrollably. "Don't open it!" Hank yelled. "Bite the end off and hold the ball in your mouth…like this!" Hank half cocked his musket and proceeded to bite the end off his charge, pour a bit of the powder into a pan near the firing device, close the cover, then dump the rest of the power down the barrel of the musket, adding the ball. He stuffed the wadding into the barrel and used the attached ramrod to drive the material deep. This took several seconds. Then he pretended to cock the rifle.

"Now you'd be ready to fire," said Hiram, who had readied his piece in the same way. "You'll want to aim at the biggest collection of red uniforms you can see; this musket is meant to shoot into the crowd. You're not hunting partridge. Don't aim; just point and pull the trigger. Soon as you fire, load again and do the same. Try for two shots a minute. And try not to notice the balls as they whistle past your own head." He smiled in a grim way.

"And mind when you shoot," added Hank. "This wet weather makes firing difficult. Your powder might not ignite with the spark."

"Then what?" asked Elijah.

"Well, you can try more powder," said Hiram, "or you can clip on the bayonet, 'cause the enemy's likely to be on you by then. I expect, too, that might be a good time to pray."

Elijah haltingly loaded his own musket, but now his arms were shaking as well. The boys continued toward the Salmon River Settlement, ever more aware of the distant explosions behind them up the lake and the occasional musketry heard up ahead, punctuated from time to time by a cannon's blast. Elijah had the urge to pull out of the group, to turn and run back the way he'd come, but he was caught up in the surge of energy that seemed to propel the group toward its destination. Plus, the woods on either side of the road were thick with giant pines—no easy way to run.

Up ahead, Elijah saw the front edge of the militia slow, and he could see the bridge at Salmon River Settlement. He braced himself, expecting to see swarms of red uniforms; he imagined soon facing what could be the end of his life. But there were no signs of open conflict, no polished ranks of red-clad soldiers—just an assemblage of ragtag looking men, some in uniform, some in typical town clothing. But muskets were held in ready position, and men were coming in and out of the tree line that framed the road leading out of the Settlement. Two cannons were in place on the bridge.

One man in a military uniform was shouting orders.

"Our scouts saw the British make a crossing, under an hour ago, north of our position, at Pike's old cantonment by the Saranac," he yelled. "General Mooers ordered us to draw the invasion force this way and lure them away from the forts—and our musket and cannon fire accomplished that goal. We aim to give them a warm welcome before they reach Salmon River. The General orders all units— military, militia, and volunteers—to take positions in these woods. Conceal yourselves behind any natural barriers you find, and fire when next you hear these cannons."

Elijah felt his breath coming in short gasps, and not just because they'd run miles so far today. Terrified, he realized the British were coming straight at them, and there was no avoiding it. Hank and Hiram dashed along the edge of the woods, paralleling the road. They saw the front of the group doing the same. There was an eerie silence, broken only by the cracking of branches as feet clattered across the uneven ground. Gone entirely was the distant rumble behind them of cannon fire from the lake. It seemed that all the action was to be before them.

Elijah glimpsed small pockets of men—militia—running back along the roadside toward them, drawing the British in. "They've seen us!" screamed one man as he ran by. "Take cover! Their vanguard is just beyond yonder turn! God, there's three battalions of the red plague, maybe four!"

"This is it, boys," said Hank. "Ready your guns. Find

a place to get off a good shot!" They skirted in among the trees, positioning themselves to see around the trees, yet not be seen. The Essex militia occupied the woods west of the road, and the Vermont militia the east side. Both were screened by trees and underbrush.

Hank, Hiram, and Elijah ducked behind a small rock hummock on the east side, in view of the road. Elijah fully cocked his musket. He dug into his ammo pouch and counted fifteen or twenty rounds prepared to fire…rounds made by Jamie the day he died. The thought crossed Elijah's mind that today might be his day to die. He wondered who might use this pouch after him. He thought about the last time he had held a gun, hunting with his brother the past spring. Now, instead of rabbits, men were his quarry. A Friend would allow himself to be killed rather than kill. How young had he been when first he'd been taught that?

Elijah's stomach felt queasy. He couldn't decide if he was hungry from lack of food these last hours, exhausted from the exertion, or so sickened by trying to be a soldier he might vomit. He stared up the road, watching, waiting for the first sign of the enemy. Something was coming. A repeating pattern of beats—drummers at the lead of the British army? His imagination? Elijah strained to listen for the approaching rhythms, widened his eyes to catch the first sight of the enemy.

There was utter silence in the woods. Elijah drew in a breath and held it, expecting to see the British front line appear from beyond the turn in the road. He knew the woods were lined with men at the ready. He wondered if his gun would fire. He wondered if he would hit anything. His shaking arms felt so weak. Hank and Hiram looked at each other, then at Elijah. They seemed calm, and Elijah tried to draw strength from them. They had been doing this for days now. They had survived. Elijah watched the road and waited.

Nothing…minutes passed. "Where are they?" said a voice from the Essex stand.

"Quiet!" issued a retort from the Vermonters across the road, and more time passed.

Then, the pounding of feet, and a small group of armed men approached down the middle of the road. Among them were several faces familiar to Elijah, and he realized they were other boys of Aikin's Company.

"The enemy column has stopped, stock-still in the road," shouted one man. "They're turning back!"

Elijah recognized Bartemus, Hazen, Freddie, and some boys whose names he didn't remember, all members of Aikin's Volunteer Company. Hank stood and asked, "What's happening, Bart?"

"Can't say," the boy replied. "Whole brigade just stopped in their tracks, sat for fifteen, twenty minutes, then started to retreat. No way of telling why. Can't see why they'd retreat back across a river they been trying to cross for a week now. The Saranac's wide and deep, with rocks so slippery it's hard to stand. Can't see them making that trip over again."

A shudder of relief overwhelmed Elijah! He would not need to use this musket after all. He wouldn't have to kill another man or be killed himself. He didn't care if the British were retreating. Let them retreat! Now he could go home. For an instant he felt God had spared him, had kept him safe. Perhaps this was the death his dreams predicted, a brush with death and nothing more. The absent God had broken through to him, protected him!

There was a commotion on the road behind them as a horse and rider approached. The horse was lathered and drooling around the bit in its mouth. Obviously it had been run hard. Elijah told himself he'd never mistreat a horse so.

"The British are reported to be in disarray," the mounted man shouted. "We are ordered to pursue their flank until we learn the reason. Chase the red beggars and give them no quarter!" He whooped and continued up the road to spread the word.

"Come on then, lads," called Hank as he and the rest of the volunteers broke into a run. "Come on, Elijah! Captain Aikin will want to meet our newest recruit." Elijah hesitated, looking back toward the Settlement, longing to join the small groups of men trudging toward the lake, to their homes, and, he guessed, to safety. "Come ON, Elijah," said Hank, coming back to pull Elijah's sleeve. "Let's give these British a good chase!" Elijah drew a deep breath. It wasn't over. Yet. For Jamie's sake, he needed to see this through to the end, whatever the end might be. He clutched his musket with both hands and ran to catch the others.

"Drive the snakes back to their holes," shouted a Vermonter not far from Elijah as he and the members of

Aikin's Volunteer Rifle Company sprinted up the woods road leading toward the Saranac River ford where the British would be retreating. The weight of the ten pound musket jarring Elijah's arms made his shoulders feel as though they were no longer attached to his body. Why pursue the British? Why not just let them go?

The road degenerated into a series of rough logging paths leading down to the river, so the militia and volunteers split apart to give pursuit. The trail opened out below them, revealing the wide, swift Saranac River cascading east, toward Plattsburgh and its terminus with Lake Champlain. The Americans kept to the edge of the woods, ready to duck into the trees if need be. As they reached the steep river bank, the seriousness of the situation became apparent.

Hundreds, perhaps a thousand, British troops in full battle regalia prowled the southern riverside, as large contingents, rifles over their heads, forded north across the swift current. Many had already made the crossing and were in formation, marching up the logging roads, away from the village. What was happening? Had they lost their bearings and suddenly headed the wrong way? Elijah began to think this might be a miracle, designed by the Almighty Himself.

Men in advance of Elijah's position began firing at the British soldiers gathered on the riverbank, felling several. The British returned musket fire, but the Americans screened themselves behind trees above the river's edge, avoiding any losses on the first volley. Hank, Hiram, and the others skirted west along the bank, keeping behind the protective pines. When they paused to fire at the rear flank of the retreating enemy, Elijah, too, pointed and fired, but was startled when his gun only gave a sickening click, with no following explosion.

Sinking to his knees, he opened the powder chamber. The powder was clotted and damp, so he shook it out, and withdrew another charge. He bit it open, poured a small quantity of powder in, then looked up as he became aware of an overpowering smell, one he recognized…the smell from his dream.

Amos Finn loomed over him, spit a wad of tobacco juice at his feet, and said, "Well, lookee here. The Quaker boy's done become a man! Yer powder's wet, boy—you be lucky they're on the run and not coming at ye." Finn loaded the gun with ease, and loped off in the direction the Aikin's boys had gone. Elijah, afraid to be alone, not knowing what to do with the rest of the charge in his hand, stuffed it into the barrel of the gun, rammed it home with the ramrod, and followed.

Unable to see Hank or the others past Finn's broad back, Elijah stayed behind as Finn ran from one tree to the next, pausing to fire and load, fire and load. Other militia nearby were doing the same. Musket blasts exploded ahead, and the sharp aroma of gunpowder clouded the air. Elijah kept telling himself he would shoot when he was sure, but he couldn't seem to bring the gun to his shoulder.

"You gonna carry that musket or use it?" Finn growled. "You get a clear shot, you take it, boy, you hear?" Elijah could only nod and wonder what had become of his friends in the Rifle Company. Perhaps they were the ones firing up ahead.

Finn stumbled and nearly fell, and Elijah, right on his heels, tripped over the body of a man whose eyes were wide open in surprise, a musket ball hole in the center of his forehead. Elijah stared, nauseated, ready to vomit. Finn grabbed the man's musket. Looking behind him, he snarled, "Get his ammo pouch. We'll need it."

Elijah gaped at the slain militiaman. By his dress, he looked to be a Vermonter. Elijah wondered if he had been among the men at the Union…how many days ago…it seemed weeks. How would this poor man's family ever know what had happened? In a flash, Elijah thought of his own family, but not for long, for Finn suddenly twisted to his right and stood, his back against a tree. With him out of the way, Elijah saw other militia behind adjacent trees, guns ready. A small company of British soldiers slipped along the river's edge, and not twenty yards ahead stood a British regular, his musket lowered at Elijah.

Muskets fired from all directions and the air billowed with smoke. Screams pierced the air, answers to the muskets' deadly roar. What voice did he hear? Was it yelling "Don't fire"…or was it "Fire!"

Elijah froze. He couldn't remember if his gun was loaded. "Shoot him, blast you," hissed Finn from behind the tree. Musket balls whizzed past his ears and thudded into nearby trees. Finn cursed and whirled to fire from behind the tree, then screamed, dropping his musket and clutching his neck. He fell back, blood draining from each side of his mouth. Elijah raised his musket and pulled the trigger. At the last instant, he saw his ramrod still poking out of the barrel of the gun. The trigger clicked, sparked, and went off with a blast. Elijah saw the blinding flash, smelled the burning hot smoke, and felt the kick against his shoulder. Instantly there was a second explosion as the gun blew apart in his hands. Everything went black around him. He saw his mother in her bed, a gentle smile on her face, his Aunt Winifred beneath the pine. He saw Jamie grin and wave his hand, walking off into a field of daisies. And then…nothing.

CHAPTER 15

Second Day, September 12, 1814

It was a strange dream, unlike Elijah's usual dreams. Inky blackness before his eyes brightened into a yellowish orange. Distant and distorted voices murmured so he couldn't understand the words. They had a hollow sound, like an old echo. But a familiar scent filled the air, and Elijah sensed he was moving. And then, all at once, he realized he was not dreaming at all. He was waking out of a sleep. But how? Why? Where was he?

His face felt odd, pulled taut, especially around his closed eyes. Elijah inhaled deeply. The sweet odor he identified as newly cut hay; the steady rocking motion coupled with the clopping sounds he knew to be a horse and wagon. But whose horse and wagon? Elijah strained to remember what could have put him in this place. He breathed in the grassy smells, feeling the scratchy hay poking into his clothing, making his skin itch. He tried to open his eyes, but they were stuck shut. He reached with his right hand to rub them, to clear them of the dry substance sealing them. His hand brushed his nose, and there was the pungent, unmistakable odor of gunpowder.

Then, he knew. The images and emotions flooded his wakening memory—running through the woods, trying to keep up, fearing he would be left alone, the image of a dead man with frozen eyes, soldiers along the river, the terror of seeing a musket pointed directly at him, an explosion and blinding flash. Elijah held his breath. He must have been captured! He must be destined for some prison compound—in Canada, far from home. He rubbed each eye gently and the flaky substance fell away. At first his blurred vision revealed nothing, but then, after blinking several times, it cleared. He looked to his left and his right, moving only his eyes. He was on his back, propped in a wagon, surrounded by piles of hay. He looked out at low, gray clouds and a long, straight road behind, somehow familiar. Elijah heard the steady drone of the wagon wheels. He decided to close his eyes, feign sleep, and try to overhear the voices that might identify his destination.

"He should be fine when he wakes up. Just some powder burns on his face is all," said a voice Elijah couldn't hear quite well enough to identify. There was a buzzing, a ringing sound in his ears.

"Seems to me he is not cut out for the soldier's life, all right," came a louder voice. "Now by the way, son, I am pleased thee would come with me. Stephen never says nothin' and it makes for a long ride."

Elijah listened in happy disbelief, recognizing the speaker as he continued: "Yes, indeed, as I said to Stephen just before we left the mill, 'Stephen,' I says, 'this boy's cut out to be a miller, pure and simple, just like I told his pa after meeting yesterday when I offered to take him as my apprentice.' And then, come to find out he has gone off to the war! Never have I seen his pa so shook up. Why, Ben Hoag, he's as stoic as they come, but he gets tears in his eyes and says to me, 'Keese, if that son of mine comes home safe, he's thine for an apprentice, and with my blessing!' When I told Stephen what had happened he got so worked up he nearly spoke!" He chuckled at his joke.

"John Keese!" said Elijah. His voice crackled and the skin around his mouth felt tight; it was hard to form the words. Plus his head pained him with each word.

"Why, Lord be praised, Henry," said John Keese, looking over his shoulder. "I believe the lad is back among us!"

Elijah strained to sit up. He pushed into the hay behind him and shoved with his feet until he was upright. Then he twisted around. His body ached as if he had worked days in the field without rest. John Keese, wearing his miller's apron, held the reins, and beside him sat Hank, from Aikin's Company. Elijah smiled, then grimaced as the skin on his face tightened and stung. He felt a hammering, throbbing, inside his head. "What has happened to me?" he said.

"Your gun exploded when you fired at that British soldier," said Hank. "You pulled the trigger and the ramrod shot out of it like an arrow and stuck in a tree—you must-a forgot and left it in when you loaded, then…Blam! The whole danged musket blew. Shards of metal and wood flew in all directions. You plumb knocked yourself out cold…plus burned your face a might. Can't imagine why that happened 'less you double loaded it."

Elijah's mind was blank when he tried to remember. The explosion seemed to be echoing still in his ears. He couldn't remember much before that, except for one thing.

"What happened to Amos Finn?" he asked.

"Dead," said Hank. "He came out from behind his tree to cover you when your gun didn't fire and took a ball to the neck. But his shot killed the redcoat."

"He…saved…me," Elijah murmured, grateful to the man who had first made him feel such revulsion, and relieved to have not killed anyone himself.

"Aye, you might say so," said Hank, "though your musket's explosion caused enough distraction we managed to overcome that company." He lowered his voice. "Can't be sure if they were trying to attack or surrender. The ones we took prisoner claimed they were trying to capture our cannon at Salmon River, but insisted they had changed their minds and were returning to their battalion. You can't trust 'em, though. Not in war."

"How did I get here?" Elijah asked.

"Well, when you didn't come to, the medics at the Settlement said you was sleeping off the shock of that blast. They treated your burns, said you'd recover. So me and the boys loaded you on a horse and I took you to Goshen. Since we met you there we thought somebody'd be able to help get you home."

"Henry found me at the mill," added John Keese. "I

was busy behind a sack of grain at the hopper when Stephen rushes in, slams down the clutch to stop the wheel. He's soft-spoken, thee knows, that Stephen, and I'd not be able to hear him with that millwheel turning. He tells me Ben Hoag's boy is stretched out across a horse out front, so I go out directly. There stands Henry to tell me the whole story. And I say, 'Praise be!' for at first day meeting the whole of the Union prayed thee might be saved, and now here thee be, thank the Lord."

The people of the Union prayed? For him? Elijah's head spun. "And the fighting?" he asked.

"Done, far as we know," said Hank. "When the British surrendered to MacDonough on the lake, the land forces retreated straight off…just turned around and headed back to Canada. That's why they quit coming at us. Today, General Macomb's order is to follow them north to make sure they don't change their minds and to pick up deserters or any of their wounded. All casualties are being taken to the hospital camp on Crab Island, American and British alike. But our company, we're all done. Disbanded today…headed back home. I said I'd bring you here; I got relations nearby. I was born in Peru, you know."

Elijah's head cleared some. Something horrible had brought him into this. What was it? And then, images: Jamie, disappearing over the bank with a wave and a smile. Jamie was dead. Angry words with his father. Sarah leaving. The feeling his life was over. Rushing to war to run away from…what? A future he couldn't believe would occur?

And now, he was alive, returning to the people who had known he was in danger, to be among friends who had come together to pray…for him. Going home. Tears of relief trickled from his eyes, washing the crusty film away, stinging his face. Cleansing tears.

"Has anyone told my father I am safe?" Elijah asked.

"Thee can tell him thyself," said John Keese. "Yonder is thy farm."

With difficulty Elijah raised himself to his knees, gripping the back of the wagon seat. There were the fields, cleared of crops, the whitewashed house with smoke drifting from the chimney, the barns. And standing between the barn and the stable was his father.

John Keese drove down the lane toward the house at a fast clip, and Elijah had to grip the seat with both hands to keep his balance. As the wagon slowed, Elijah wobbled to his feet, still clutching the backrest. He saw his father's jaw drop open, his eyes widen, his face break into a smile. Ben Hoag let go of the basket of eggs he was holding and began to run. "My dear Lord!" he boomed. "Molly! Rebecca! Jeremiah! Elijah has come home to us!" Elijah couldn't help thinking how fast he ran, for a big man.

Ben leaped up the spokes of the wheel before the wagon stopped and gathered Elijah into his arms as if he were a little boy. He stepped down, still holding Elijah, and the warmth of his embrace filled Elijah with such joy and relief that the pain of the horrible memories, his pounding head, the ache of his body—melted away. Elijah turned to see Rebecca approach, supporting their mother on her arm. Jeremiah, whooping and hollering, sprinted from the paddock. Tears streamed down their faces. Elijah leaned back against his father as they pressed into him and hugged him, all three, all at once. He felt his mother's tender fingers brush his face and the skin around his eyes. "Soon we shall have thee healed," she whispered.

"I am healed now," said Elijah, feeling such happiness and peace he could no longer hold back his tears. For the first time in days he felt safe. "Pa," he said, turning back to his father and embracing him, "I am sorry…sorry for all I've done to hurt thee."

"Elijah, it's not thee who need apologize," Ben said, hugging him again.

"Well, now I'd say it's time we take our leave, Henry," said John Keese. "God be praised for this happy reunion!" He turned to address Ben. "Whenever the boy is ready, Ben Hoag, he can begin the apprenticeship if it's of interest to him." Elijah waited for the negative reaction from his father, but instead Ben smiled and nodded.

"After his time of healing, if he's a mind to," said Ben, extending his hand to the miller. "I'm grateful to thee for bringing my son home."

"'Tis the Lord who brought him home," said John Keese, "thanks to the strong petitions of a community come together in the Light. I provided the horse and wagon, is all!"

"Yes," said Ben. "Truly the Lord's doing." For once, Elijah did not doubt it.

"We're off then," said John Keese. He snapped the reins and turned the horses and the wagon in the yard, heading them up the drive. "Stephen will be out on the front steps, waiting. He's not fond of the hopper! 'Tis why I need thee, Elijah Hoag," John Keese shouted over his shoulder, "and sooner than later!"

"Our thanks for helping my son, young man," called Ben.

Hank leaned over the back rest and waved. "Perhaps we'll see each other again!" he said, as the wagon clattered up the drive and swept out onto the Rogers Road. The Hoags stood a moment in silence, watching. They could see John Keese, holding the reins in one hand, gesturing with the other.

"John Keese loves to talk," said Ben, smiling. "A fact thee will learn soon enough, being with him every day." He paused. "He's a good man."

"Thee are truly giving me thy blessing to be John Keese's apprentice?" Elijah asked. "What of the farm?"

"I know it to be the right thing. As for the farm, with thee gone, and Israel gone, the work will fall to Jeremiah and me." Ben dropped a huge hand on Jeremiah's shoulder and squeezed. Jeremiah reddened, but returned his father's gaze, smiling broadly.

"There will be times when I may help thee," offered Elijah. "The mill is not active every season."

"I would not want to distract thee from thy responsibility to John Keese," Ben said.

"I can hold more than one job," Elijah said. "Many Friends are farmers first, but have other skills—blacksmiths, house joiners, wheelwrights. Why, thee are a stockman and have done carpentry and have worked on leather harnesses, for thyself and others." Elijah had never addressed his father in this way, as one adult to another. "John Keese is a farmer as well. I can help thee when need be while learning the miller's trade."

Ben looked at Elijah, his eyes softening. "Thy leaving taught me many lessons," Ben said. "I saw how I have controlled thee, how I have ignored thy desires for thy own life. I forgot how when I was a youth I shunned skills offered to me by my uncles, skills that would have taken me from the farm work I loved. I felt God's call to the farm. I lost sight of how thee are becoming a young man, possessing your own mind, hearing your own call. When Israel told us of his decision, I was desperate that thee stay here, happy or not. My desperation blinded me. Now thy friend is dead, Elijah. His family is leaving…the girl is leaving with them." Ben shook his head. "I was wrong not to help them in their grief. I realized this through my own grief at losing Israel, and then the thought of losing thee. God be merciful to the Greens…and to me."

"I shall never forget Jamie, or his family, or Sarah. But my life is here in the Peru Union. My dreams assure me," Elijah said.

"Dreams?" asked Ben. Elijah hesitated, and looked off toward the hills.

"Tell him, Elijah," said his mother.

Elijah met his father's gaze. "For months I've had dreams like the ones Cousin Joseph had. Aunt Winifred believes they are like hers and Cousin Joseph's."

Ben stroked his beard. "And these dreams…have they come to pass?"

"Yes," said Elijah, "in everything I've lived through these last days. I know now I love this place more than I imagined, and I would be lost without it, without my family. I am no farmer, but I believe I can be a miller and stay among the Friends."

"Where does thee think these dreams come from?" asked Ben.

"God," answered Elijah, more sure of it than ever before. "In the quiet, when I tried to go to the Light, my head was filled with images I couldn't understand. I saw them as obstacles, but now I believe God has reached out to me in the dreams all along. They are a blessing, my pathway to the Light."

Ben smiled. "Praise the Lord, who once again bestows a gift upon this family. And I thought Israel…" His voice drifted off.

"Must he be disowned, Pa?" asked Elijah.

"It is the law of the community. Being apart from the world helps us retain purity of thought and belief." Ben Hoag stared at the ground, kicking the earth. "Ah, but it was so much easier to judge when our family was not involved. Since Israel refuses to reconsider, the meeting has voted to disown him. Until living it, I'd never understood how one's heart can break."

"Israel will always be my brother." said Elijah. "I will not disown him in my heart. I do not care what the meeting decides."

"Nor shall I," said Jeremiah.

"Nor shall any of us," said Ben. "He shall ever be our son, your brother, but he must remain apart."

"Can you do nothing as overseer to change the position of the community?" Elijah asked.

"I made it known to the meeting yesterday I would no longer accept the role of overseer," said Ben. "I see how my concern with legalities caused me to lose sight of the most important things in my life. I was so possessed by laws and rules I believed my thoughts were God's. I know otherwise now. I cannot change the things I have said, the hurt I have inflicted, but I am different, thee will see. I shall use my energy for the benefit of the family I love. Thy mother is healed. I believe it is a sign of a new beginning for us."

"Thee has always been a man of great faith, Benjamin. That truth has been constant," said Molly Hoag. "It is what drew us together."

"Look, Elijah!" said Rebecca. "There are others who want to welcome thee home."

"Who?" asked Elijah, wondering if it might be Aunt Winifred and her sister. "There," said Rebecca, gesturing down the drive toward the paddock.

Two by two, a dozen or so of the young cows were plodding up the driveway toward the family, wagging their heads and bawling their welcome.

"Merciful God," cried Ben. "Who left that paddock gate open? Eli—? *Jeremiah*?"

"Don't worry, Pa," said Jeremiah, running toward the herd. "I'll round them up."

"Not alone, thee won't," roared Ben, starting after him. "Can thee help, Elijah?"

"I can try," said Elijah, following after his father, feeling suddenly stronger, inexplicably energized. Rebecca's peal of laughter followed him as he caught one of the smaller calves by the nose and turned it around. Jeremiah was shoving the stragglers back into the paddock. Ben rushed into the herd, scooping up a calf in his arms.

Elijah grinned and shook his head. He couldn't help thinking how fast his father ran, for a big man.

AFTERWORD

Readers of historical fiction might wonder which parts of a story are history and which parts are fiction. Authors of historical fiction hope they have made it difficult to tell!

Among Friends is set during the Battle of Plattsburgh in the waning years of the War of 1812. The invasion by the British down the Lake Champlain valley of New York State was intended to regain territory lost in the Revolutionary War by cutting off most of New England from the rest of the country. Although peace talks were already going on in Europe, the area would have no doubt been annexed by Canada and returned to British rule had they won the battle.

The day by day time line of the story events follows the historic record. A journal written by Henry K. Averill, who at the time of the battles was a teenage member of a group of boys who banded together as Aikin's Volunteer Rifle Company, contributed additional detail. Henry was "Hank" in the story, the main spokesman for the group of boys. All the names of the Aikin's company used in the story refer to the actual members, including Peters, the only one recorded as killed.

The details of the Battle at Culver Hill as described by David Cochran in the story follow the historic record and Averill's journal; indeed, the Peru Militia, led by Cochran, was one of the first units to engage the advancing British line. The military leaders mentioned throughout the story—Generals Macomb and Mooers, Colonel Appling, Commodore MacDonough—were real people whose military expertise along with a good bit of luck brought about a successful ending to what might have been a rout by the British.

The Yellow Store in the small settlement of Goshen where Elijah first meets Aikin's Volunteers was a real establishment, and Asa Elmore was the man who ran a dry goods store in Peru Village. The relationship between Asa's daughter and Israel Hoag is imagined, although many a Quaker from the Peru Union married "world's people," and were disowned, helping lead to the dissolution of the Union.

Today, little remains of the Peru Union, the first main settlement in the township. One of the Quaker meetinghouses is a home. A few houses from the period stand along the Union (once Rogers) Road. The cemetery is there. But farm fields fill the place once home to forty-five houses, stores, a school, a post office, an inn, and other typical town structures of the time.

The Union was settled by Quaker immigrants from Duchess County and Long Island. William Keese came in 1789 and built a log home there. Two years later he was followed by his father (John III) and brothers Richard, John, Stephen, and Oliver, who established farms. Stephen eventually had a son, John, who with his father operated the Keese, Rogers, and Keese Sawmill at Goshen by 1805. Among Friends depicts John and Stephen as brothers. The Keeses also operated a grist-mill, as described in the book. Their personalities and interactions are fictional, although the story about how Stephen and John Keese brought the millstone up Lake Champlain in the winter from Long Island is part of the local lore.

The character Elijah Hoag is fictional, though an Elijah Hoag did live at the Union in the years following the war. A David Hoag did live at the Union during the war period. Joseph Hoag, from Ferrisburg, reportedly had visions predicting strife among the Friends, political developments, the effect of slavery—even the civil war. His vision was reported in pamphlets and in New York City newspapers.

Elias Hicks was a Long Island farmer who travelled the region preaching his ideas, as described by Elijah's mother in the story. His preaching led to a division among Quakers in 1827. Many Peru Quakers hailed from Ferrisburgh, VT, and there is record of Hicks's visit there in the early 1800's. His relationship to the characters is imagined, but his impact on the Peru Union was real. The community divided in the early 1820's, building a second meeting house for the Orthodox Quakers. The followers of Hicks, Hicksites, remained in the original building. Seeds of the conflict can be seen in the interaction between Samuel Green and Benjamin Hoag. Many Peru Quakers did leave the fellowship for the Short Creek Meeting in Ohio, perhaps in search of fertile western lands, but also to get away from fellow Quakers with whom they differed.

The author used writings by the notable local writer J.W. Harkness, who produced many articles about Old Peru in the late 1800s. These articles were compiled and edited at the time of Peru's Bicentennial celebration in 1992 in a book by Lincoln Sunderland. *Reminiscences and Early History of Old Peru*, a collection written by members of the Peru Grange (1913), was very helpful in identifying names of famous local citizens and the places they lived. Of course, the Journal of Henry K. Averill, transcribed and published by Keith Herkalo in 2001, particularly the account of the movements of the Aikin's Volunteer Rife Company, served as overlay to the fictional events in the life of Elijah Hoag.

Well known books of local history, found in the bibliography, served as sourcebooks for the historical events of the week leading up to September 11, 1814. Other volumes there listed gave background in Quaker belief and lifestyle. They would be useful to anyone seeking additional reading on the subject.

BIBLIOGRAPHY

Brinton, Howard. *Friends for 300 Years.*
Wallingford, PA: Pendle Hill Publications, 1994.

Everest, Alan S. *The War of 1812 in the Champlain Valley.*
Syracuse, NY: Syracuse University Press, 1981 (1st printing).

Hamm, Thomas D. *The Transformation of American Quakerism.*
Bloomington and Indianapolis: Indiana University Press, 1992

Herkalo, Keith. *The Battles At Plattsburgh: September 11, 1814.*
New York: The History Press, 2012.

Herkalo, Keith, ed. *The Journal of H.K. Averill, Sr.*
Plattsburgh, NY: Studley Printing and Publishing, 2001

Whitmore, Catherine. *Plain Living.*
Notre Dame, IN: Sorin Books, 2001.

ABOUT THE AUTHOR

Stephen B. Woodruff is a retired Elementary school teacher, having taught grades 4-6 during his thirty-two-year career. He has published several articles and a story for children's magazines, and authored two books, both biographical commentaries in a series called *Money At Its Best: Millionaires of the Bible* (Mason Crest, 2009): *Noah* and *Esther*.

He holds Bachelors and Masters of Science degrees from the State University of New York at Plattsburgh, and attended Princeton Theological Seminary from 1977 to 1978.

He lives near Plattsburgh with his wife and three children. In his spare time, he enjoys woodworking, singing in choirs, and playing organ and banjo.